A special Merry Christmas from Superromance
and
***New York Times* bestselling author**

DEBBIE MACOMBER

Turn on the Christmas tree lights,
relax and enjoy this brand-new story about that
irrepressible angelic trio, Shirley, Goodness and Mercy.
This story celebrates the meaning of family—and the
power of love. It's a Christmas fantasy about
people who are very real, people you'll come
to care about, people you'll want to visit again.

When you finish *Those Christmas Angels,*
you'll put the book down with a smile on your face…
and a sigh of satisfaction.

Because what would Christmas be without
Mercy and Goodness? (And don't forget Shirley!)

"Popular romance author Debbie Macomber
has a gift for evoking the emotions
that are at the heart of the genre's popularity."
—*Publishers Weekly*

Dear Reader,

For years, I wrote for Harlequin and Silhouette's romance series. When I was a young wife and mother, romance novels were what I read. That was back in the days when I was potty training four kids at the same time and was desperately in need of stories with happy endings! Come to think of it, I still am. That's what's universal about romance and why women of every generation have treasured these stories.

Twenty-five years ago, I decided I wanted to write romances, too. With little more than a high school education and a burning desire to be a writer, I rented a typewriter and pounded out my own stories. Five years and four completed manuscripts later, I sold my first book. As they say, the rest is history—and what a wonderful history it's been, thanks to Harlequin and Silhouette.

It was among the faithful romance readers that I gained my first audience. My early fans have been my foundation and my constant support. This Christmas story featuring Shirley, Goodness and Mercy, my first full-length Superromance novel, is my thank-you gift to you. Enjoy their madcap adventures this holiday season. I hope my three angels will warm your heart and put you in the Christmas spirit.

As always, I love to hear from my readers. You can reach me through my Web site (www.debbiemacomber.com) and leave a message in the guest book or write me at P.O. Box 1458, Port Orchard, WA 98366.

Merry Christmas!

Debbie Macomber

DEBBIE MACOMBER

THOSE CHRISTMAS ANGELS

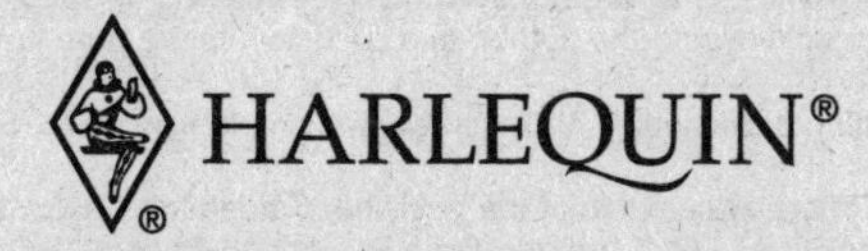

TORONTO • NEW YORK • LONDON
AMSTERDAM • PARIS • SYDNEY • HAMBURG
STOCKHOLM • ATHENS • TOKYO • MILAN • MADRID
PRAGUE • WARSAW • BUDAPEST • AUCKLAND

ISBN 0-373-71164-6

THOSE CHRISTMAS ANGELS

This edition published by arrangement with Harlequin Books S.A.

Visit us at www.eHarlequin.com

Printed in U.S.A.

In memory of Sandy Canfield,
talented writer and dear friend.

And to Charles Canfield with affection and thanks
for the 38 years of love and support
he gave Sandy.

CHAPTER ONE

ANNE FLETCHER pulled the last box of Christmas decorations from the closet in the spare bedroom. She loved Christmas—always had and always would, regardless of her circumstances. It was a bit early yet, a few days before Thanksgiving, but some Christmas cheer was exactly what she needed to get her mind off her problems. The grief that had been hounding her since the divorce… The financial uncertainty she now faced… The betrayal she still felt…

"No," she said aloud, refusing to allow herself to step closer to that swamp of regrets. It often happened like this. She'd start thinking about everything she'd lost, and before she knew it, she'd collapse emotionally, drowning in pain.

Carrying the plastic container down the hallway, she glanced inside her art room and paused to let her gaze drift over to her easel and her latest project. The bold colors of the setting sun against the backdrop of the Pacific Ocean pleased her. Yes, she was divorced, but there'd been compensations, too. Her art had fulfilled her in ways she hadn't even recognized were possible.

How different her life was at fifty-nine than she would've imagined as few as five years ago. What Burton had done was unforgivable. He'd hurt her—and cheated her of funds that were rightfully hers.

Once again she stopped herself, not wanting to indulge those bitter memories and regrets. She'd done plenty of that in the beginning, when she'd first learned he'd found someone else and wanted out of their thirty-year marriage. It was a fling, or so she'd managed to convince herself. A midlife crisis like the ones so many men suffered. Any day Burton would come to his senses and see what he was doing to her and to Roy, their son.

Only he hadn't, and Anne walked out of divorce court numb with shock and disbelief. Not until the judge's gavel echoed through the room had she fully believed her husband was capable of such treachery. She should've known, should've been prepared. Burton was a top-notch divorce attorney, a persuasive man who knew all the ploys. But despite everything, she'd trusted him....

Her friends had been stunned, too—less by Burton's deception than by Anne's apparent acceptance of what he'd done to her. It wasn't in her to fight, to drag her marriage and her life through the courts. Burton had recommended an attorney, whom she'd obediently retained, never suspecting that the man who'd represented her in court would apply to Burton's law firm as soon as the divorce was final. Of course, he'd been hired....

Burton had promised to treat her fairly. Because she was convinced that he'd soon recognize what a terrible mistake he was making, she'd blindly followed his lead. Without a quibble and on her attorney's advice, she'd accepted the settlement offer—one that had turned out to be grossly unfair. Without realizing it at the time, Anne was cheated out of thousands of dollars' worth of assets.

Burton's ploy in this particular case had been simple: he'd strung her along. Twice he'd come to her in tears, begging her forgiveness, talking about reconciliation, and all the while he'd been shifting their assets to offshore accounts. All the while, he'd been lying, stealing and cheating. She'd loved him and she'd believed him, and so had taken her husband at his word. Never had she dreamed he could betray her like this. After thirty years, she'd walked away with only a pittance. And, needless to say, no alimony.

Yes, Anne could fight him, could take him back to court and expose him for the thief he was, but to what end? It was best, she'd decided long ago, to preserve her dignity. She'd always felt that life had a symmetry to it, a way of righting wrongs, and that somehow, eventually, God would restore to her the things she'd lost. It was this belief that had gotten her past the bitterness and indignation.

Anne refused to be bitter. At this point, she couldn't see how anger, even righteous anger, could possibly help her. She'd adjusted. Taking the little she'd managed to salvage from her marriage, she'd purchased a small cottage on St. Gabriel, a tiny San Juan island in Puget Sound. In college all those years ago, when she'd met Burton, she'd been an art student. She had a flair for art and enjoyed it. Given the demands of being the wife of a prominent divorce lawyer, she'd put aside her own pursuits to assist Burton. Her husband's ambitions had become her own, and Anne was the perfect wife and hostess.

It'd been a disappointment to her to have only one child, a son they'd named after Anne's father. Roy was the light of her life, her ray of sunshine through the years. When she wasn't hostessing social events on her husband's behalf, Anne spent her time with Roy, raising him with limitless love and motherly devotion.

If there was any bitterness in her soul about the way Burton had treated her, it was for what he'd done to Roy. Unfortunately, Roy was the one who'd introduced Burton to Aimee. He never forgave himself for that, despite Anne's reassurances. Still, Roy took on the blame and assumed responsibility for what had followed. He couldn't seem to forgive himself for his role in the divorce, no matter how innocent that role might have been.

To complicate the situation even more, her son refused to forgive his father, not only for betraying Anne but for stealing Aimee, the woman he himself had loved and planned to marry. Roy's anger was constantly with him. The anger had become part of him, tainting his life, as though he wore smudged, dark glasses that revealed a bleak, drab world. All Roy cared about now was his business, his drive for more and more, and while he'd achieved greater success than most men twice his age, Roy wasn't happy.

Her son's cynicism troubled Anne deeply—even more than the divorce itself. She'd put that behind her, as much as she was able, and built a comfortable life for herself, doing what she loved best—painting. Mostly through word of mouth, her work had started to sell at the local farmers' market and then at a couple of galleries in the area; it now provided her with a small income.

Anne would've given anything to help her son. No matter how much money he made or how many accolades he received, he remained lonely and embittered. She desperately wanted him to find happiness.

In the five years since the divorce, Roy had not spoken to his father once, despite Burton's repeated efforts. Yet Roy was so like Burton. He shared his father's talents, his ambition. They shared another trait, too, the one that concerned Anne the most. Roy possessed his father's ability to be ruthless, but he'd directed that ruthlessness primarily at marriage and relationships. Roy was thirty-three, and in Anne's view, he should get married. However, her son resolutely refused to discuss it. His attitude toward love and commitment had been completely warped. He no longer dated, no longer sought out relationships.

The only thing that mattered to Roy was the bottom line. He'd grown cold and uncaring; little outside of Fletcher Industries seemed to affect him. Anne realized her son was in trouble. He was hurting badly, although he seemed incapable of recognizing his own pain. Roy needed someone to teach him the power of forgiveness and love. She'd wanted to be that person, to show him that forgiveness was possible, but in his zeal to succeed, Roy had started to block her out of his life. It was unintentional, she knew, but nonetheless, it hurt.

Roy had established Fletcher Industries, his own computer security company, shortly after he graduated from college in Seattle. His innovative, cutting-edge software led the competition in the field. Recent contracts with the government and several banks had given Fletcher Industries a solid position as one of the top companies of its type.

Those first years after his business was formed, Roy spent far too many hours at work, caught up in the wave of demand. It wasn't uncommon for him to stay in the office for two or three days at a time, living on fast food and catnaps. That all changed after he met Aimee. Her son had fallen in love and he'd fallen hard. Anne had been thrilled and Burton was, too. Then Roy had brought Aimee to his home in Southern California to introduce her to his parents, and all their lives had exploded.

Following his parents' divorce, Roy had quickly reverted to his old habit of working long hours. Only now a callousness had entered into his business dealings. Anne was aware of this, but she was helpless to change her son, and her heart ached with her inability to reach him. Time and again, she'd tried to open his eyes to what he was becoming, but he couldn't or wouldn't hear.

The kettle whistled, and leaving the Christmas box in the hall, Anne moved into the kitchen. She took the blue ceramic teapot from the cupboard and filled it with boiling water, then added a tea bag—Earl Grey, her favorite—and left it to steep. After a moment, she poured herself a cup and took a first sip of the aromatic tea. She frowned, berating herself for allowing her thoughts to follow the path they'd taken. Just when she assumed she was free of Burton, she'd wallow in the pain all over again and realize how far she had yet to go. There was only one cure for this bout of self-pity and for the worry that consumed her. Setting down the china cup, Anne bowed her head and prayed. Sometimes it was difficult to find the words to express what was in her heart, but not today. The prayer flew from her lips.

''Dear Lord, send my son a woman to love. One who'll help him heal, who'll teach him about forgiveness. A woman who'll open his heart and wake him up to the kind of man he's becoming.''

Slowly, as if weighed down by her doubts, Anne's

prayer circled the room. Gradually it ascended, rising with the steam from the teapot, spiraling upward out of the simple cottage and toward the leaden sky. It rose higher and higher until it reached the clouds and then sped toward the heavens. There, it landed on the desk of the Archangel Gabriel, the same Archangel who'd delivered the good news of God's love to a humble Jewish maiden more than two thousand years ago.

Gabriel, however, was away from his desk.

Shirley, Goodness and Mercy, three Prayer Ambassadors who had a reputation for employing unorthodox means to achieve their ends, stood just inside the Archangel's quarters. Together the three of them watched as the prayer made its way onto his desk. Only the most difficult prayer requests went to the mighty Archangel—the prayers that came from those who were most in need, from the desperate and discouraged.

"Don't read it," Shirley cried when Goodness, unable to resist, bent to pick up the wispy sheet.

"Why not?" Goodness had always had more curiosity than was good for her. She knew that peeking at a prayer request before Gabriel had a chance to view it was asking for trouble, but that didn't stop her. Mercy was the one most easily swayed by things on Earth, and Shirley, well, Shirley was nearly perfect. At one time she'd been a Guardian Angel but had transferred to the ranks of the Prayer Ambassadors. That had happened under suspicious circumstances, so Shirley's perfection was a little compromised. Shirley never mentioned the incident, though, and Goodness dared not inquire. She knew that some things were better left unknown—despite her desire to hear all the sordid details.

"Goodness," Shirley warned again.

"I'm just going to glance at the name," Goodness muttered, carefully lifting the edges of the folded sheet and peeking at the signature.

"Is it anyone we know?" Mercy demanded, drawing closer.

Goodness eyed Shirley, who was doing her best not to reveal her own interest. "Well, is it?" Shirley finally asked.

"No," Goodness said. "I've never heard of Anne Fletcher, have you?"

"Anne Fletcher?" Shirley cried, and then as if her knees had gone out from under her, she sank into the chair reserved for Gabriel. "Anne Fletcher from California," the former Guardian Angel repeated slowly.

Goodness looked again, lifting the edge of the sheet just a bit higher this time. "Formerly of California," she said.

"Oh, no!" Shirley cried. "She moved. I wonder why. Tell me where she's gone."

"The San Juan Islands," Mercy said, bending over Goodness to take a look for herself.

"She's in the Caribbean?" Shirley said, sounding distraught.

"No, in Puget Sound—Washington State," Goodness told her.

"I remember it well," Mercy said with a dreamy smile. "Don't you remember the Bremerton Shipyard? We had so much fun there."

"What I remember," Goodness informed her angelic sister, "was all the trouble *we* got in when *you* started shifting aircraft carriers and destroyers around."

"I don't know how many times you want me to apologize for that," Mercy muttered, crossing her arms defiantly. "It was a fluke. Nothing like that's happened since, and frankly I think you're…"

Her words faded as she saw Goodness studying Shirley. "How do you know Anne Fletcher?" Goodness asked softly.

"Poor, poor Anne," Shirley murmured, seemingly lost in thought. "I knew her mother—I was her Guardian Angel. I was with Beth when she gave birth to Anne."

So Shirley had a connection to Anne Fletcher. "I didn't read the request," Goodness said, more eager than ever to throw caution to the winds and take a second, longer look.

"Maybe there's something we can do," Mercy said. It sounded as if she was encouraging Goodness to flout protocol, and Goodness was happy to go along with the implied suggestion. She quickly scooped up the prayer request, then almost dropped it when a voice boomed behind them.

''Do for whom?'' it asked.

Gabriel. The Archangel Gabriel.

Goodness spun around and backed against the side of the huge desk, crushing her wings in her eagerness to hide. Oh, this wasn't good. Gabriel was their friend, but he wouldn't tolerate their snooping around his desk.

''Nothing.'' Mercy moved closer to Goodness until they stood shoulder to shoulder, wing to wing.

Shirley remained lost in her own thoughts, sitting in Gabriel's chair, apparently oblivious to their dire circumstances.

''Do?'' Goodness choked out. ''Are we supposed to be doing something for someone?''

''It's Anne Fletcher,'' Shirley whispered, peering up at the Archangel, apparently still in a stupor. ''We've got to help her.''

''Anne Fletcher?'' Gabriel repeated. His brow furrowed with concern.

''She's said a prayer for Roy,'' Goodness explained, and boldly handed Gabriel the request, as much as admitting it had been read. ''She *wants* to believe. But she's worried about her son and has given up hope that anyone can reach him. We can't let her lose faith—we just can't!'' She gazed up at Gabriel with large, pleading eyes. Her wings were folded back in place and she hung her head as if she felt the same sense of despair as Anne Fletcher.

Goodness had never seen Shirley so upset. Clearly this Anne person was someone she cared about.

Gabriel made a grumbling sound. Shirley glanced up and with a look of panic realized she was sitting in the Archangel's chair. She bolted upright, then leaped to one side.

It was such a rare sight to see Shirley ruffled that, had she not felt so worried about her friend, Goodness would've been amused.

Once his chair was vacant, Gabriel sat down, ignoring the prayer request. Instead, he reached for the massive book from the shelf behind him. With a soft grunt, he set it in front of him. He opened it to the section marked F, and ran his finger down a long list of names inscribed there.

Goodness knew better than to stand on tiptoe and take a peek. Even she understood when it was best to restrain her curiosity.

"Anne Fletcher," Gabriel said thoughtfully. "It's been five years since the divorce."

"Anne's divorced?" Shirley whispered. "Oh, my, I didn't know. How's she doing?"

"Actually, quite well," Gabriel told her. "She's adjusted far better than we'd expected." The Archangel nodded. "She's gone back to her art and that's helped her. It says here that she's living in Washington State, on a small island in Puget Sound."

"Burton always discounted her talent," Shirley said, and leaned on her palms against the desk, daring to read the huge volume that documented human lives. "She could've been a successful artist had she continued her studies."

"Still might," Goodness threw in as if she was in the know. She *hated* being left in the dark when it came to earthly matters. Humans had always intrigued her. They were the very pinnacle of God's creation, fearfully and wonderfully made, yet so obtuse. It was hard to believe free will could cause such problems.

"Anne Fletcher is indeed talented," Gabriel murmured, "but fame and fortune were never important to her. She's had to deal with various losses, but as you already know, for every loss there is an equal gain. Often humans have to search for it, though."

Goodness nodded in full agreement, although she couldn't begin to guess what God had in store for the fifty-nine-year-old divorced woman. "God has another man for her, doesn't He?" she ventured.

Gabriel frowned as if Goodness's comments were starting to irritate him. "No, Goodness, not another man. Frankly, Anne isn't interested."

"I don't blame her for that," Mercy tossed in. "After what Burton did to her, she'd find it very difficult to trust again, and who could blame her?" She nodded as if that was all anyone needed to say on *that* subject.

"The prayer is for her son," Gabriel pointed out as he read the request.

"Roy," Shirley said. "You remember Roy, don't you?" she asked mournfully. "He was such a sweet child, so willing to please, so anxious to follow in his father's footsteps."

"Burton never forgave him for not pursuing a law degree," Gabriel commented in an absent sort of way. "Roy is gifted, but he works too hard."

"I'm sure Anne would like grandchildren," Shirley said, studying the prayer request.

"Of course she would," Mercy agreed.

For the first time since they'd entered the room, Shirley smiled. "God provides," she whispered, and then said in a louder voice, "Isn't that what you were just saying?"

Gabriel glanced up. "Roy isn't interested in marriage."

"Not now he isn't," Goodness chimed in. The possibility of romance rose before her—it was such fun to steer humans toward one another! Creating romance was by far her favorite duty on Earth.

"We want in on this," Goodness announced.

Gabriel leveled a fierce gaze on her, and she swallowed hard and took a step back.

"Only if you think it's for the best, though," she mumbled.

"It's for Anne," Shirley pleaded. "Beth's little Annie."

"Are you saying the three of you want to return to Earth?"

Shirley, Goodness and Mercy all nodded simultaneously.

"I was afraid of that." Gabriel stroked his chin. "I don't think Earth has recovered from your last visit yet."

''We'll be exceptionally good this time,'' Mercy promised, folding her hands as if in prayer. ''I swear I won't even *think* about going near an escalator.''

''It isn't moving staircases that worry me,'' Gabriel said. ''It's everything else.''

Goodness stepped forward again. She could tell by the look in his eyes that Gabriel was weakening. ''We can help her, Gabe.''

''Gabe?'' he bellowed.

''Gabriel,'' she corrected swiftly. ''I know we can. Besides, I have this romance thing down pat. Humans are eager to fall in love. All we've got to do is lead them in the right dir—'' She stopped when she saw Gabriel's expression.

For a long moment, no one spoke and then in a low whisper, Shirley said, ''Please?''

Gabriel took his time answering while Goodness waited, holding her breath in anticipation. She was eager to see Earth again. They'd been away far too long—several Earth years at least.

Oh, Gabriel, make up your mind, she muttered to herself. *Say yes!*

CHAPTER TWO

ROY FLETCHER hated doing job interviews. He warily regarded the older man sitting on the other side of his desk. Dean Wilcoff had to be close to sixty and retirement. His thinning gray hair was brushed away from his face and his dark eyes squarely met Roy's. He was big, an inch or two over six feet, broad-shouldered and muscular. He'd obviously maintained himself physically, which was good. As head of building security, it was unlikely he'd be chasing intruders, but he should at least be capable if the need arose. Roy glanced over Wilcoff's résumé a second time. The man had an impressive work history.

"You were with Boeing's security force for twenty-six years."

"I was," Dean answered without elaborating. There'd been some downsizing at the airplane manufacturer, but Roy guessed that Dean Wilcoff had left or been let go for another reason. Still, his Human Resources Department had selected this candidate for him to interview.

The dates on Wilcoff's résumé showed that he'd last worked nine months ago, yet Roy didn't sense any desperation in the man. Wilcoff should be worried. By now, his unemployment benefits would've expired and at his age, obtaining another job wouldn't be easy.

"What do you know about computers?"

For the first time Roy noticed hesitation in the other man. "Only enough to get around on the Internet. My daughter's been after me to take one of those courses, but frankly I don't see the need. I work security. It's what I know and what I do best. If you hire me, Mr. Fletcher, you can rest assured that no one's going to break into your office, day or night."

Roy raised a skeptical eyebrow. Life didn't come with guarantees. Everything was suspect. Everything and everyone. This was a lesson he'd learned the hard way, but learn it he had.

"I'll get back to you," he said, dismissing the man. He'd finished the round of interviews and although all the candidates were qualified, there hadn't been a single one he especially liked. The day before, he'd talked to three applicants, and three more today. No one had really impressed him. Unfortunately he needed to make his decision soon if he didn't want hourly phone calls from his HR director. Well, fine. He'd put the names in a hat and simply draw one. At this point, that was as logical a way to handle the situation as any.

"HOW'D IT GO?" Julie Wilcoff asked her father as she set the salad on the dinner table. She hated to ask, but he hadn't exactly been free with details since his return from the long-awaited interview. Julie was afraid that meant bad news, and he'd already had enough disappointments. After nine months without a job, her father had grown restless and discouraged. She knew he was worried, especially with the holidays so close. He'd wanted to have a new job lined up by New Year's, and he'd had such hope for this one, which seemed perfect for him. Yet he'd barely said a word since he'd come home from the interview.

"Why hire an old man like me?" he muttered as he walked to the table.

"Because you're highly qualified, dependable and intelligent."

"I'm not even sure I want to work for Roy Fletcher," her father complained. He pulled out his chair and sat down.

Julie frowned. After weeks of searching, of making a half-dozen unsuccessful applications, after talking up this interview for days on end, his attitude came as a shock. But if her father, a man who never exaggerated or jumped to conclusions, made such a statement, there was a reason.

Roy Fletcher's name had appeared in the media for years. He was the genius behind the security software business, the man entrusted by the government to keep out hackers. Fletcher Industries had prospered as doing business online had become increasingly prone to theft—of credit-card numbers, private information, financial records and more. Her father was in security, too, only a different kind. While Roy Fletcher made sure no one could break into computer files, her father prevented intruders from breaking into the doors and windows of buildings.

Julie sat down at the table and handed her father the meat loaf. It'd been her mother's recipe and remained one of his favorite meals. Julie had hoped this would be a celebration dinner, but apparently not. Still, she wondered what had prompted her father's comment. "What's wrong with Mr. Fletcher?" she asked.

"I don't much care for him."

"Mr. Fletcher interviewed you himself?" Dad hadn't mentioned that earlier.

Her father nodded. "After I talked to a nice gal in what they call Human Resources." He paused a moment. "She sent me to see him." Another pause. "He isn't a pleasant man."

Julie scooped up a serving of scalloped potatoes and put them on her plate. Toward the end of her mother's final bout with cancer, Julie had moved out of her apartment and back in with her parents. Her father had quit his job and stayed home to nurse her mother. His company benefits had paid most of the medical bills; Julie's salary as a junior-high physical-education teacher covered the rest. It had been a time of sacrifice for them all. Letty, Julie's fraternal twin, had helped, financially and emotionally, as much as possible, although she no longer lived in Seattle.

After six months of this arrangement, Julie's beautiful, petite mother had died. That was four months ago. From the beginning, the doctors had given them little hope. Julie, Letty and their father knew and were prepared for the eventuality of Darlene Wilcoff's death. Or so they'd assumed. What Julie had learned, and her sister, too, was that it didn't matter how ready you thought you were to face the death of a loved one; even when death is expected, it hits hard. Letty, Julie and their father had been left reeling. It felt to Julie as if her life would never be the same—and it wouldn't be. The world had lost a graceful, charming soul; she and Letty had lost a loving mother; Dean had been deprived of the woman he adored.

Julie waited until their plates were filled before she questioned him again. "What exactly didn't you like about Roy Fletcher?"

"He's cold." Dean hesitated and his brows drew together. "It's as if nothing touches him, nothing affects him. From what I've heard, people don't mean much to Fletcher. In fact, the whole time I was with him, I had the feeling there wasn't a single person in this world who meant a damn thing to him. I doubt he's an easy man to know."

"People usually have a reason for acting the way they do," Julie said, hoping that would encourage her father to continue the conversation. She couldn't help being curious. The job offered an employment package that was far above anything he would have received with another employer.

He agreed, but then added, "I got the impression that Fletcher thinks everything boils down to money, but there are some things that can't be bought."

Julie nodded.

Her father sampled the meat loaf, then set down his fork. "It's time, you know."

Julie pretended she didn't understand, but this was a discussion they'd had more than once. Her father seemed to believe Julie should move back into an apartment of her own, now that her mother was gone. She disagreed. First, her father needed her. Oh, he'd muddle through with meals and housework; Julie had no doubt of that. But she knew he was lonely and struggling with an all-consuming grief. As well, finances were tight, and it went against his pride to let someone, even his daughter, pay the bills.

What he didn't grasp—and she could find no way to explain—was how badly she needed to be with him. They'd suffered the biggest loss of their lives, and being together seemed to help. She wasn't ready to move out. Eventually she would, but not yet. For her, it was still too soon.

"We've already been through this."

"And your point is?"

"Now, Dad, Letty and I think—"

"You should have your own life, instead of taking care of your old man."

"I do have my own life," she insisted. "I'll stay here until we're both back on our feet. Then you can kick me out."

"The thing is, I might never get back on my feet, especially financially," he said, his gaze dark and brooding. "It's time we faced facts here. I should sell the house."

"No!" Julie cried, the thought unbearable. Losing the family home so soon after her mother's death was more than she could accept emotionally. Not if there was any way to stop it. "Letty and I refuse to let that happen."

Letty wanted to help more, but as a young navy wife, she lived in Florida with two small children. Her husband was periodically at sea, sometimes for months at a time. Although twins, Julie and Letty were about as different as two sisters could be. Letty was like their mother, small and delicate, with blue eyes and wavy blond hair. A classic beauty. Julie took after her father's side of the family. Her hair and eyes were a deep shade of brown. Tall, strong and solidly built, she was a natural athlete. She'd played center in basketball, pitcher in softball and was a track star all through high school and college.

While boys had flocked around Letty, they'd mostly ignored her sister. Letty had brains, as well as looks, and although Julie had brains, too, she wasn't pretty the way her sister was. It had never bothered her until recently, when she realized she was thirty years old. Her sister was married, and so were most of her friends. Sure, she dated, but the number of eligible men had dwindled as the years went on. With her mother growing increasingly ill, Julie hadn't worried about it much. But now… She sighed. Like her father in his job search, Julie had given up hope of meeting the right man. For a girl over thirty, the pickings were slim.

The phone rang, and Julie and her father both turned to stare at it.

"Let the machine pick it up," he said. That had been a hard and fast rule during her teenage years—no telephone call was worth disrupting family time at the dinner table.

"You sure?" Julie asked.

Her father nodded and continued eating. "You did a good job on the meat loaf."

"It's Mom's recipe, remember?"

Her father grinned. "It might surprise you to learn she got it from a 'Dear Abby' column."

The phone rang again. "No way!" This was news to Julie.

Her father chuckled. "That broccoli salad I like came out of the newspaper, too."

Her mother had never told her this, but then it was Letty who usually hung around the kitchen. Julie was always at basketball practice or some sporting event. There'd been so many things her mother had never had the opportunity to tell her. Unimportant things, like this, and other things—revelations, advice—that really mattered. How Julie wished she could go back and recapture all those precious hours with her mother. If only she'd known…

The answering machine clicked on and they heard a disgruntled male voice. "This is Roy Fletcher."

Without thinking, Julie launched herself toward the phone, whipping the receiver off the cradle before Fletcher could end the call. "Hello," she gasped. "I assume you want to speak to my father?"

"Yes, if your father is Dean Wilcoff."

Her dad was right; the man's voice was devoid of the slightest warmth.

"Just a moment," she said, handing him the receiver.

"Dean Wilcoff," he said gruffly, frowning at Julie. His look said that if it'd been up to him, he would've left Roy Fletcher cooling his heels. Fortunately Julie had been closest to the phone.

She bit her lower lip as she studied her father. This *had* to be good news. Roy Fletcher wouldn't phone to tell a man he'd chosen another candidate for the job.

Her father's eyes widened. "Before I accept the position, I have a few questions."

Julie wanted to wave her arms over her head and scream. Her father needed this job and not only for financial reasons. *Oh, Dad, don't blow this now.* It was too important.

After what seemed an eternity, her father slowly replaced the receiver.

Julie could barely contain her anxiety. "Well?"

"I'm seeing Mr. Fletcher in the morning to discuss my questions." The smallest hint of a smile touched his mouth. "For better or worse, it looks like I've got the job if I want it."

"Oh, Dad! That's terrific news."

"That, my dear Julie, remains to be seen."

CHAPTER THREE

"WOULD YOU CARE to meet Anne Fletcher for yourselves?" Gabriel asked, eyeing the trio.

Goodness couldn't believe their good fortune. She nodded and smiled as Mercy eagerly agreed. It'd been so long since they'd last visited Earth with its manifold delights. The place was definitely interesting—and appealing—but completely unlike Heaven with its gold-paved streets. Earth was also dangerous, full of exotic allures and various temptations. Heaven, on the other hand...well, eyes hadn't seen or ears heard all that awaited those in glory.

Shirley's face brightened. "Could we visit for just a little while? I haven't seen her in years."

"At one time Anne routinely prayed for her son," Gabriel explained as he guided them out of his quarters and to a convenient location to view Anne's little spot on Earth. "For a long while after the divorce, she brought Roy's hardened heart to God's attention, but when she didn't see results, her faith weakened. Now only an infrequent prayer comes our way."

"That doesn't surprise me," Shirley whispered. "When I was assigned to her mother..." She paused and looked up guiltily, as if afraid she'd said more than permissible. "I'm sure all Anne really wants is for her son to be happy."

"But happiness is a condition of the mind, not circumstances," Gabriel reminded them. "That appears to be a most difficult lesson for humans. They expect to find happiness in things, which we all know is impossible." Sadly he shook his head. "They repeatedly fail to see what should be perfectly logical."

"Humans require a lot of patience," Goodness said, doing her best to sound knowledgeable.

Gabriel studied the trio, as if gauging how much he could trust them if he did grant them passage back to Earth. Goodness did her utmost to look serene and confident. She fully intended to be good, but she couldn't count on Mercy. Shirley was iffy, too. Her friend appeared to have a special fondness for Anne, and there was no telling what she'd do once they arrived on Earth.

Goodness didn't begrudge the Archangel his doubts. The trio always left Heaven with the best intentions, but once they began to mingle with humans, their powers to resist grew increasingly weak. They found it difficult not to interfere in situations that hadn't been assigned to them—which inevitably got them into trouble.

Gabriel's gaze was drawn back to the big blue sphere, the view of Earth from Heaven.

Goodness peered closer but wasn't able to make

out anything yet. Gabriel would need to bring everything into focus.

"Yes, I'm afraid that where it concerns her son, Anne's lost hope," the Archangel murmured sadly. "She doesn't understand that some things need to be believed in order to be seen."

Goodness was impressed. "That's so wise."

"Poor Anne," Shirley murmured, her brow wrinkled in worry.

"We can help her, I'm sure," Mercy insisted, sidling next to Shirley. "Anne needs us." She glanced from Gabriel to Shirley, looking for confirmation.

Goodness bit her tongue to keep from chastising her friend. They couldn't act too eager, otherwise Gabriel might become suspicious. He might wonder if they had ulterior motives for wanting to visit Earth. As unobtrusively as possible, she made a small waving motion with her hand, hoping Mercy would get the message.

"Of course," Mercy added with an exaggerated sigh, "there are any number of angels more qualified than the three of us."

"Yes, there are," Gabriel said bluntly.

"I thought you said we could see her from here," Shirley said, squinting through the thick cloud cover.

For a moment Gabriel seemed to be having second thoughts. His expression became more severe as he stared at them. Little wonder humans were terrified of Gabriel, Goodness thought. His imposing seven-foot stature was enough to intimidate the bravest of men. That was one reason, she supposed, that he was only sent from Heaven on the most serious of missions.

Slowly he raised his massive arms and with one sweeping motion the clouds cleared and the mist gradually thinned, revealing the small cottage surrounded by tall fir trees. Then Anne came into view. She stood in her art room, a paintbrush in her hand. A few Christmas decorations hung here and there, as if a halfhearted effort had been made to display them.

Once more Shirley leaned forward, peering downward anxiously. ''Anne's painting,'' she said, and pointed to the scene below.

Once the mist faded completely, Goodness stepped closer to her friends to get a better look. Just as Shirley had declared, Anne Fletcher stood in front of an easel, apparently deep in thought.

Goodness examined the painting and was pleasantly surprised. Shirley had been right; the woman was a talented artist. She used bold, distinctive colors and strong, confident lines. Despite the beauty of her landscape, Anne was obviously dissatisfied. She seemed about to paint over the canvas and destroy her work. Instead, she set her brush and palette aside and slumped into a chair. Tilting her chin, Anne stared at the ceiling, blinking back tears.

''What's wrong?'' Shirley demanded, turning to

Gabriel for an explanation. "She looks like she's going to cry."

"She's worrying about her son," Gabriel said. "She—"

"But she's prayed for him," Shirley broke in. "Anne knows to leave matters with God. Her mother taught her the importance of trusting in God," she said. "But that was so long ago...."

"She spoke to her son a little while ago, and things are even worse than she realized. She's given up all hope."

"But she *prayed*—how can you say that?" Shirley demanded. "After everything she's been through, after all she's suffered. Look," she cried, gesturing at the weeping woman, "there's no bitterness or hatred in her, no ill will toward Burton and his new wife."

"That's true," Gabriel agreed, and he seemed truly amazed by the simple human act of forgiveness. "Anne has forgiven her husband for what he did to her, but she feels helpless to influence her son."

"Why is God taking so long to answer?" Shirley asked, pacing restlessly.

"He has His reasons. It's not for us to second-guess the Creator of the Universe."

For an instant, it seemed as if Shirley was about to argue, but Goodness intervened. "Perhaps God was waiting for the right woman to come along. A woman who'll open Roy's eyes—and his heart. It can't be an ordinary woman, but one strong-willed enough to stand up to his arrogance.''

''But who could that be?'' Mercy asked, looking wide-eyed at Gabriel.

''This woman is waiting to be found, and I'm sending you to Earth to find her.''

''We're going back?'' Goodness hadn't been convinced that Gabriel would actually agree, since he so obviously had reservations about their dependability. She was thrilled. And right before Christmas, too! Oh yes, this was excellent news, the best yet.

''Yes, you may go,'' Gabriel said in a guarded voice, ''but with a few stipulations. You have less than a month—the prayer request must be answered before Christmas Eve, and in the process your goal is to teach these humans a lesson. Can you do it?''

''We can,'' Shirley promised.

''We'll be better than ever,'' Mercy insisted.

''I'll keep an eye on them both,'' Goodness assured the Archangel.

''But who will watch you?'' he asked, cocking one dark brow.

Goodness sputtered, hardly knowing how to respond, then straightened. She recited her mission statement. ''I...I will faithfully fulfill my duties as an Ambassador of the Almighty.''

''Well said.'' Gabriel nodded with approval, but Goodness wasn't fooled. One wrong move, and the three of them would be jerked back from Earth with its multitude of fascinating distractions.

A short while later, they'd all gathered in Anne Fletcher's art room. It was a small area with plenty of light. Canvasses were stacked against the wall, some painted, others a pristine white, waiting to come to life. Anne sat near a phone with a cup of tea in her hand. After a long moment, she reached for the phone.

"Who's she calling?" Mercy asked.

"Shh," Goodness warned. Thankfully, Anne wasn't aware of their presence nor could she hear their voices, unless special arrangements had been made well in advance. They were required to go to Gabriel for permission to reveal themselves—but there were inventive ways around that.

"Listen," Shirley said, hushing them all.

ANNE PUNCHED OUT the private number to Roy's office. There was no guarantee that he'd speak to her. She didn't doubt that he loved her, but her son was avoiding her these days. Anne wasn't fooled; she knew why he did this. While she tried not to nag him, Anne realized she must sound like a distant echo, repeating the same message. No wonder he looked for ways to sidetrack her—or avoid her altogether.

"Roy Fletcher," came his gruff, disembodied voice.

"It's your mother," she said with a cheerful lilt. "I haven't heard from you in so long." Immediately she wanted to bite her tongue. This wasn't how she'd intended to start their conversation. Why, oh, why had she said that? It must have sounded like a chastisement, and that was the last thing she wanted Roy to think. "But I know how busy you are," she said, faltering a little.

"Do you need anything?" he asked, already sounding bored. He'd be quick to write a check, and had on several occasions, although she'd never cashed one. She wondered if he was aware of that. It wasn't Roy's money she wanted, it was his happiness. No amount of money he gave or received, no matter how generous, could buy that.

"I'm fine, Roy. And you?"

"Busy."

"Are you telling me you can't talk now?" Or any other time, she thought, disheartened.

He hesitated. "I have five minutes."

Anne almost had the feeling he was setting a timer. "I called to tell you I'm coming into Seattle next Thursday." The trip required a ferry crossing and a half-hour drive; it often took a couple of hours to make the journey across Puget Sound.

"Any particular reason?"

"I'm meeting Marta Rosenberg for dinner."

"Should I know the name?" Roy asked.

Anne sighed, resigned now to his lack of interest and enthusiasm. Except for his work, everything in life seemed to be an effort for Roy.

"There's no reason you should remember the name," she told him. "Marta and I were good friends in college. We've kept in touch through the years—Christmas cards, that sort of thing. She's made a real name for herself in New York as an art dealer."

Surprisingly, that piqued his interest. "Is she going to sell your paintings?"

"Oh, hardly," Anne said, embarrassed at the idea. Anne would never approach her friend with such a request. Her paintings were amateurish compared to the work Marta sold, work by big names. Revered artists. "I was hoping you and I could meet beforehand," Anne suggested. She wanted to get to her main reason for calling before her allotted time elapsed.

"I have a half hour open at lunchtime," Roy murmured.

Anne's spirits lifted. "That would be lovely. I'm meeting Marta at seven and—"

"I'll pencil you in for noon. I have a meeting and I might be a few minutes late, so don't be upset if you're left twiddling your thumbs for a while."

"I was thinking I might decorate the windows at your office before Christmas," she hurriedly added.

Her remark was followed by a lengthy pause. "You want to do what?"

"Paint your windows, you know, for Christmas."

"Is this a joke, Mother?"

"No, it'll add a festive air to the complex. I was thinking of those big windows in the front lobby. In case you hadn't noticed, 'tis the season, Roy. Don't you remember how we used to paint the windows at the house every year?''

Again his response was slow and edged with sadness. ''Of course I remember, but I was a kid then. I've outgrown things like that.''

Anne didn't feel that way in the least. She wanted to do whatever she could to resurrect happy memories for him. ''You won't mind, though, will you?''

''If it pleases you, then by all means paint.'' His voice softened slightly. ''I have to go.''

''I know.'' Her five minutes was all used up.

''I can't promise you lunch, but I'll do my best to squeeze you in.'' With that, the phone line went dead.

Anne set the receiver back in its cradle as if it weighed thirty pounds.

''IF HE CAN SQUEEZE her in!'' Mercy cried, outraged. ''This is worse than I thought. Anne's his *mother!* How are we ever going to find a woman willing to put up with that kind of behavior?''

Actually, Roy Fletcher was in worse shape than anyone had thought, Goodness mused. They had their work cut out for them.

''Oh, dear, look,'' Shirley whispered.

Anne Fletcher's hand remained on the telephone, as if she was trying to maintain an illusion of contact with her son. Her head fell forward and her shoulders slouched. Suddenly, before the other angels could react, Shirley slipped into the middle of the room.

"What are you doing?" Goodness demanded, reaching out unsuccessfully to stop her.

"Anne needs encouragement," Shirley insisted. "She can't continue like this."

"You're going to get us pulled off this assignment," Mercy warned. "We haven't been on Earth five minutes. That's a record even for us."

"Don't you remember what Gabriel said?"

"Darn straight I do! One wrong move and we're out of here."

"No," Shirley countered, "he said some things had to be *believed* in order to be *seen.*"

"But he didn't say for us to leap in and do something we know isn't allowed."

Mercy's warning, however, went unheeded. "What's Shirley going to do?" she asked Goodness.

"I'm afraid to find out," Goodness replied.

"I'm going to prove to Anne that she *should* believe," Shirley announced grandly.

"But that's the opposite of what Gabriel meant," Mercy argued.

"I'm doing it," Shirley insisted.

Sure enough, she stepped through the thin layer of truth that separated angels from humans. For a moment she did nothing but soak in the earthly environment. Then, in a display of heavenly grace, the angel unfolded her wings, extending them to their complete and glorious length. With the full splendor of the Lord reflecting upon her, she revealed herself to Anne.

Anne Fletcher gasped and placed her hand over her mouth. To her credit, the human seemed suitably impressed. Slowly Anne dropped her hand and stared hard at Shirley, as if she expected her to disappear. She blinked once and then again, obviously testing to see if this could possibly be her imagination. Anne shaded her eyes from the light. Then, still staring, she reached for a pad and pencil and started to sketch.

"Oh, no."

Mercy looked around, certain they were about to lose all visitation rights until the next millennium. Nothing happened.

Seconds later, Shirley was back. Goodness forced herself to keep quiet and not reprimand her friend. Mercy had no such restraint.

"How could you?" she wailed.

"Anne needed a sign," Shirley said, "and I gave it to her. God is working, and I wanted her to know that—to believe."

"But look what she's doing!" Mercy cried, watching as Anne worked on the sketch, her fingers moving at a furious pace as if she was struggling to get everything she'd seen down on paper before it faded from memory.

Goodness could hardly wait until Gabriel heard about *this*.

CHAPTER FOUR

JULIE WAS PROUD of her father, and so pleased that he'd been granted this opportunity. Abraham Lincoln Junior High where she taught was only a short distance from Fletcher Industries. The first day he was scheduled to work, she suggested she ride in with him and then pedal her bike from the complex to the school. It was hard to find opportunities to exercise, and this seemed a good solution, in addition to giving her extra time with her father every morning. Folding a change of clothes into her backpack, she dressed in her spandex pants and nylon shirt. She attached her bicycle to the carrier on the rear of the Ford, then joined her father in the front seat.

"Are you excited?" she asked. If he wasn't, *she* certainly was. Her father could use a psychological boost. It'd been a long dry spell for both of them.

He shrugged.

"Well, I am." It felt, in some strange, inexplicable way, as if they could finally begin to heal—that their time of grieving was about to end. Not that either of them would forget Darlene Wilcoff. She was alive in their hearts and would forever remain a part of them. Now, four months following her death, this crisp, clear late-November morning seemed filled with renewed promise.

"You're sure about this bicycle business?" her father muttered as he started the engine. "I don't like the idea of you riding home in the dark."

"It's perfectly safe, Dad," she said, half-tempted to say that at thirty, she was well beyond the age of needing parental supervision. "I'm wearing a helmet and a vest that reflects in the dark, plus the bike has a flashing light in the front and the back."

He grunted as if he still disapproved, but didn't argue further. As they reached Fletcher Industries, her father slowed. "You'll need to be here at five this afternoon."

"I will." That would allow her time to finish up some paperwork and cycle back to the complex. "Where would you like me to meet you?"

He frowned as if he hadn't considered this earlier. "In front of the building would probably be best. The parking lot is a secure area and I don't want you going in there without me."

"Great. I'll see you at five."

Her father pulled close to the tall office building and put his car in park while Julie climbed out. Other cars had already started to arrive, and a delivery truck circled toward the back of the complex.

Julie walked around to the rear of the Ford and removed her ten-speed. Her father drove off once he'd pointed out where they should meet. His taillights disappeared as he turned the corner and drove toward the employees' designated parking area, joining a line of other vehicles.

Julie had just finished snapping the helmet strap under her chin when a sharp male voice spoke from somewhere behind her. She whirled around.

"What's your business here?" Oh, great, her father's first day and she was going to have a confrontation with a security guard.

"Hello," she said, smiling warmly. "I'm Julie Wilcoff. My father—"

"I asked you to state your business."

The man was no guard, Julie could now see. He was tall, an inch or two more than her five foot eleven, and dressed in a dark suit, expensive, judging by the cut, although she didn't have a discerning eye when it came to fashion. He might have been handsome, but scowling as he was, he appeared intimidating and in no mood for excuses.

"I'm on my way to school."

His expression implied that she was lying.

"You're not a student."

"No, I'm a teacher. My father dropped me off here to show me where I should meet him tonight when he's finished work. Are you Roy Fletcher?" This could be the man her father had described; his attitude certainly resembled that of the company owner.

The man ignored her question. "Your father is Dean Wilcoff?"

"Yes." She had to bite back the urge to call him *sir.* It'd been a long time since any man had intimidated her, and she wasn't about to let it show. "I didn't realize there were rules against riding bicycles in this complex."

"There aren't. Be on your way," he ordered, starting toward the front door.

Julie planted one hand on her hip and glared at him. "I beg your pardon," she said in her best schoolteacher voice. How dare he speak to her like this!

He paused, and then with exaggerated patience, said, "You're free to go."

"In case you're unaware of it, I was entitled to do so before." No wonder her father had taken a dislike to Mr. High-and-Mighty. He was, without exception, the most disagreeable person she'd ever met. His arrogance was absolutely staggering.

He ignored her and walked into the building.

Fuming, Julie climbed on her bike and locked her cleats into the pedals. She rode hard, her anger driving her faster and faster as she left the complex and then merged with traffic on the main thoroughfare outside Fletcher Industries. She arrived at Abraham Lincoln a good ten minutes earlier than she'd estimated. She parked her bicycle, still muttering to herself, and carefully removed her helmet.

"Mornin'," Penny Angelo, who taught English,

said cheerfully as she passed the bicycle rack, briefcase in hand.

Julie managed a halfhearted greeting and then added, her outrage flaring back to life, "You wouldn't *believe* what just happened."

"Did you cross paths with a rude driver?" Penny guessed, eyeing her ten-speed.

"No, a tyrant!" Julie waited for her heart to stop pounding and exhaled slowly in an effort to regain perspective. She refused to allow the encounter to affect the rest of her day. "It's behind me now," she said, making a determined effort to put Roy Fletcher out of her mind. If indeed it *had* been him. He hadn't answered her question, but she could only assume she'd run headlong into the company's owner.

Despite her rough start that morning, Julie had a good day. She enjoyed teaching; she was strict but fair, and her students understood that and respected her for it. After her last class, Julie changed out of her work clothes and back into her cycling gear and pedaled the five miles to Fletcher Industries.

Invigorated, she arrived at the spot her father had suggested they meet. She hadn't been there more than a few minutes when a uniformed guard approached. It seemed she was destined for trouble. Probably Mr. Nose-in-the-Air had ordered him to chase her off. Well, if that was the case, she was ready. She had every right to be there, and she intended to let him know it.

"Ms. Wilcoff?" the young man asked politely. His name tag read Jason.

She relaxed her stance. "Yes?"

"Your father said he'd be a few minutes and asked that you meet him in his office."

"Oh, okay."

"I'll show you up."

What a difference from the way she'd been greeted that morning! The guard indicated where she could park her bike and then led her into the building. Entering the elevator, dressed as she was, Julie felt a bit self-conscious. She smiled shyly at a couple of women and decided that perhaps this bike-riding business wasn't the best idea, after all, especially if she was going to be meeting people. She'd give it a week and see how it went.

Her father's office was on the third floor. He looked up and smiled when she came into the room. "How was your day?"

"Great," she said, dropping into a chair. "How about yours?"

"Fine, fine. I won't be more than a few minutes." He didn't look up from the computer screen, which he studied intently. "Just checking some employee records," he murmured. "I'm getting the hang of this computer stuff now."

"Take your time, I'm in no hurry."

"Wilcoff." The same unfriendly voice that had almost ruined her morning sounded from the doorway.

Julie turned her head to find the same unfriendly man—presumably Roy Fletcher. His eyes narrowed when he saw her.

"You again?" he said.

Her father rose and cast a glance from his employer to Julie. "This is my daughter, Julie. You've met?"

"I had the pleasure this morning." Fletcher held out his hand.

They exchanged brief handshakes. "Pleasure isn't exactly the word I'd use," Julie primly informed him.

"You teach English?"

"No," she returned in a clipped voice. "Etiquette."

The merest hint of a smile touched his mouth. "I see."

"Julie teaches physical education, Mr. Fletcher," her father corrected, apparently surprised she'd claim otherwise.

Fletcher ignored her and focused his attention on Dean. "I wanted to let you know my mother's stopping by sometime this month to paint a decorative Christmas scene on the front-lobby windows." He frowned as if he disapproved. "She seems to think some Christmas cheer will put me in the holiday mood," he said with heavy sarcasm.

Julie doubted he was interested in goodwill, now or at any other time of the year.

"I'll make sure no one bothers Mrs. Fletcher," her father assured him.

"I'd appreciate it." He turned to go, then changed his mind. "How was your first day?"

Her father hesitated. "Challenging."

"Good, glad to hear it." With that, Fletcher was gone as fast as he'd appeared.

"Good, glad to hear it," Julie repeated, and rolled her eyes. "Is that the most unpleasant man you've ever met in your life or what?"

"He's my employer, Julie, and he has more important matters on his mind than either you or me."

"How can you defend him?" she cried. "You said he was cold, but I had no idea he was *this* cold."

"He has a lot of responsibilities," her father insisted. "I've only been with the company one day, but I can see that people respect him, which says a great deal. There has to be a reason the staff feels like that about him."

If her father wanted to defend the tyrant, fine. She wasn't going to argue with him.

"I wonder what made him like this," she murmured while her father cleared off his desk. She didn't expect an answer and he didn't give her one. Perhaps eventually she'd learn more about Roy Fletcher. Then again, perhaps she wouldn't. Because Julie didn't care if she ever saw him again.

"IT'S HER," MERCY SHOUTED joyously, clapping her hands with delight. "She's the woman we've been sent to find for Anne's son."

"Who?" Shirley asked, looking around the empty office.

"Julie, of course," Mercy said irritably. "Dean Wilcoff's daughter." Mercy seemed disappointed that they didn't see things as plainly as she did.

"Julie? This Julie?" Goodness repeated, incredulous. "Get out of here!" Julie Wilcoff wasn't at all like the kind of woman she had in mind. Besides, anyone could see those two had started off on the wrong foot. Julie openly disliked the man. His feelings were harder to read, but she wouldn't be surprised if Roy had trouble remembering Julie's name two minutes after they'd met.

"Open your eyes," Mercy insisted, sitting on the file cabinet in Wilcoff's darkened office. "They're *perfect* for each other."

Shirley remained skeptical. "Sorry, I just can't picture it."

"Me, neither," Goodness concurred. She tried her best to imagine them as a couple. They didn't fit together, somehow. They both had strong personalities that would constantly collide. Goodness thought a gentle, loving woman would be better suited to the likes of Roy Fletcher. Someone soft and quiet. Someone less opinionated, more compromising. They hadn't found this paragon yet, but give them time and they would. Of course, they didn't *have* a lot of time. Their assignment on Earth was limited to a short three weeks.

"Am I the only one here with a brain?" Mercy groaned. "Julie's the right woman because she isn't going to let him intimidate her. She's got the strength of will to stand up to him, and he'll respect her for that."

"True," Shirley reluctantly agreed. "I don't mean to be unkind here, but have you noticed that...well, Julie's a very sweet girl, but..."

"She's a woman with all the right qualifications."

"Yes, of course, but, well, she's rather...large."

"I believe the term Shirley is looking for," Goodness said, stepping forward, "is big-boned."

"She's tall and she's...solid," Mercy said forcefully. "Don't forget, she played sports all those years. She's not some skinny little size-two model type."

"I know you mean well," Goodness said, not wanting any more distractions from the matter at hand, "but Anne's son is handsome and wealthy, and frankly, as we're all aware, he can have any woman he wants."

"He knows that," Mercy said, "and he doesn't care."

"Aimee was blond and beautiful," Shirley said as though reading Goodness's mind.

"How do you know that?"

"I...peeked at the file on Gabriel's desk when no one was around."

"You did *what?*" Goodness burst out.

''It doesn't matter what Aimee looks like,'' Mercy insisted. ''Okay, so she was blond and cute. Didn't work out, though, did it?''

''Obviously not,'' Goodness said grudgingly.

''Do you think he's still in love with her?'' Shirley asked.

''I doubt it.'' Although Goodness couldn't know for sure, she suspected that Roy had put Aimee completely out of his mind—her and every other woman in the universe.

This was what made their mission so difficult. It was up to the three of them to find Roy a woman who would warm his cold, empty heart and teach him about love. No wonder Gabriel had warned them. This was perhaps their most difficult assignment to date.

''I like Julie,'' Mercy whispered.

''She's apple pandowdy and Fletcher wants cheesecake,'' Goodness said, proud of her analogy.

''He's had cheesecake.'' Shirley shot upward to join Mercy, crowding next to her on the filing cabinet. ''I'm beginning to think Mercy's right. Roy's lost his taste for the exotic. He needs a woman with substance, a woman who's truly his equal.''

Goodness thought perhaps her fellow Prayer Ambassadors had a point, but convincing Roy wouldn't be easy. ''Just how are we going to persuade him to give Julie a second look?''

''And what about Julie?'' Shirley demanded. ''She didn't exactly fall for *him* at first sight.''

''I think you're right,'' Goodness said. ''Roy might need a bit of angelic assistance, but Julie's going to be even harder to convince.''

''Oh, dear, I hadn't thought of that,'' Mercy muttered. ''She's taken a rather keen dislike to him, hasn't she.''

''That can be fixed, too.''

Goodness and Mercy turned to look at their friend. ''What do you mean?''

Shirley chortled happily. ''Why don't I show you, instead?''

CHAPTER FIVE

"I HATE THE IDEA of you having to work on a Saturday," Julie said as her father prepared to walk out the door. He'd already explained that it was because of the Thanksgiving holiday that had just passed.

"I don't mind. There's a lot to do." She watched him go and realized it'd been a very long time since she'd seen her father content. After only a few days, she was aware of what this new job had done for him. Once again, Julie was grateful that he'd been given this chance to prove himself. Despite her personal feelings about Fletcher, whom she considered both rude and egotistical, she appreciated the faith he'd placed in her father. Her sister agreed. They exchanged daily e-mails; Letty had told Julie she was encouraged by the changes she already saw in their father and suggested Julie make an effort to get along with the "big boss" if she saw him again—which she probably wouldn't.

Julie leaned against the door and sighed after her father had left for work. A sigh of relief, of satisfaction. Looking heavenward, she whispered, "We're going to be all right, Mom. We're moving ahead with our lives.'' Deep in her heart, she knew her mother heard her and approved.

The surprising thing Julie had learned in the past year was that life does go on. Despite her loss, despite her pain, Julie had come to understand that. Clichéd as it sounded, it was true. She was pulled, against every dictate of her will, into each new day. Gradually, as she resumed her routines and her habits, it became easier. This didn't mean she missed her mother any less or had stopped thinking about her—that would've been impossible—but life continued.

After showering and doing a few house-cleaning tasks, Julie tackled the kitchen. It was when she opened the refrigerator that she noticed her father's lunch. He'd forgotten it. Knowing he'd go without rather than pick up something easy, she dialed his work number. When he wasn't available, she asked the man who answered to please let her father know she'd deliver his lunch later that morning.

As she left the house, Julie decided this was the perfect opportunity to get in some exercise. Soon she'd start training for the STP, the annual two-hundred-mile bicycle ride between Seattle and Portland, Oregon. The two-day event was held every July and she'd participated in it faithfully until her mother's illness. Julie had skipped the past two years, but was eager to get back into a regular training program.

Dressed in her biking gear, she wheeled her ten-speed out of the garage and placed her father's lunch in one of the paniers over the rear wheels. Then she headed for Fletcher Industries. It felt good to work hard, to pump her legs and exercise her lungs. At top speed she turned off the busy road and into the long driveway that led to Fletcher Industries. In the small mirror attached to her helmet, she noticed a black sedan pulling in behind her. The driveway was narrow and there wasn't room for her to move over to allow the vehicle to pass. Leaning forward as far as she could, her arms braced against the handlebars, Julie reached maximum speed, forcing her legs to pedal even faster.

Obviously the sedan's driver hadn't seen her. Julie gasped as the black vehicle hit her rear tire. The collision sent her hurtling through the air, arms flailing. Her heart stopped when she realized there was no way to avoid missing a fir tree. A scream froze in her throat. If her head slammed against the tree at this speed, helmet or not, she'd be a goner. The last thought she had before impact was a fervent hope that her father not be the one to identify her body.

Then she landed.

It was as though she'd collided with a pile of pillows. Following impact with the tree, she fell on her backside with a solid thump. Too stunned to react, Julie sat there. By any law of nature, she should be badly injured.

Only, she wasn't. In fact, she seemed to be unscathed. Surely that was impossible!

"Are you all right?"

A pale, shaken Roy Fletcher stood above her. Equally shaken, Julie looked up at him and blinked several times, unable to find her tongue.

"I should be dead," she whispered, and thrust out her hand, assuming he'd help her up.

"You should be arrested for pulling a stunt like that," he said angrily, ignoring her hand. "Stay put until I can get an ambulance and the police." He reached for his cell phone and frantically started punching numbers.

He wanted her arrested. Of all the nerve! "Listen here," she cried, still in a sitting position. "*You* were the one who ran into me."

"You're insane!" He was shouting now. "Not you," he said into the tiny cell phone and clicked it off. "I didn't touch you." He stared down at her, a puzzled look on his face. "I can't believe you're not hurt."

"I'm fine...I think."

"That was the most idiotic stunt I've ever seen. Why did you do it?"

"Me?" *He'd* run into her. And here he was yelling at her when the entire accident had been his fault. "Do you honestly think I voluntarily flew through the air and collided with a tree?"

He shook his head and rubbed his eyes as though

to clear his vision. "I don't know what the hell just happened, but I didn't hit you."

"Fine. Whatever. Just help me up." She extended her arm to him a second time. Shaky as she felt, she needed the assistance.

"No!" He raised both hands. "Stay put," he said again. "You could've broken something and don't know it."

"I'd know it," she muttered. While she admitted to being shaken, she wasn't about to let him bully her. Although the trip to her feet lacked grace, she was soon upright.

"Don't move," he said again. "Wait for the paramedics."

"I'm perfectly all right," she insisted, removing her helmet.

"You can't be sure of that. Now do as I say and stay where you are."

"Would you kindly be quiet and stop giving me orders?" Disgruntled, she brushed the dirt from her backside. So far, so good. Nothing even ached. She could see no scrapes, no bruises.

Fletcher shook his head again, his expression one of hopelessness. "Are you always this unreasonable?"

Examining her ten-speed, Julie wanted to weep. It was ruined. "If you didn't hit me, how did this happen?" she cried, angry now. If he planned to claim his car hadn't touched her bike, she had evidence that said otherwise.

''If you hit that tree, why aren't you injured?'' he snapped.

Julie didn't have an answer for him anymore than he did for her. They stood glaring at each other, unwilling to back down, when the ambulance, siren blaring, rounded the corner.

Before she could protest, two paramedics had her sitting down. While Fletcher explained what had happened, Julie, under protest, was placed on a stretcher. ''Would someone please listen to me,'' she said as she struggled to sit up. ''I'm fine. I don't even have any bruises. I'm not hurt.''

The taller of the two paramedics picked up her dented helmet. ''You hit that tree?'' he asked, and it sounded as if he didn't believe her.

''I saw it with my own eyes,'' Fletcher confirmed.

''He saw it because he ran into me,'' Julie immediately said. He wasn't an innocent bystander in this accident. He'd caused it.

''My car didn't touch her bike.''

By this time, the police had arrived, and an officer pulled up behind the ambulance. Fletcher scowled at her as if to say this was all her fault, but *he'd* contacted the authorities. She hadn't wanted to. While the police talked to Fletcher, Julie answered the paramedics' questions. When they suggested she be checked out at the hospital, she refused.

''Look,'' she said, dismissing their concern, ''I'm none the worse for wear.'' The last thing she wanted was to arrive at the hospital in an ambulance when she wasn't even hurt.

"You'll have your own doctor examine you?" the second man asked.

"I will," she promised.

"I'll see that she does," Fletcher added.

The policeman knelt down in front of Fletcher's sedan. "I don't see any marks here."

Fletcher looked at Julie, his eyes full of suspicion. "I don't know how to explain what happened, but I swear I didn't hit you."

"Would you stop telling me how innocent you are?" Then it dawned on her that he was afraid she was going to sue him. As a man with deep pockets, he'd be worried about lawsuits.

"I don't see any evidence here," the police officer said, frowning in puzzlement.

Men always stick together, Julie thought irritably. Well, if that was what the police had decided, so be it.

"We'll leave it for you two to settle," the patrolman said.

"Thank you," Roy told him.

The paramedics climbed back into their vehicle and drove off, and shortly afterward the police car followed.

"Look at my bike!" Julie studied the damage to her ten-speed. The entire back wheel was bent and twisted; the frame had buckled beyond repair.

"I'll buy you another," Fletcher said as he placed her crumpled bike in the trunk of his car.

"So you *are* admitting responsibility," she challenged, hands on her hips.

"No," he said in a flat, businesslike tone.

"You don't have to worry, you know. I have no intention of suing you."

He didn't respond as he opened the passenger door. "Get in," he said curtly.

"Where are you taking me?"

"To my personal physician."

"I said I'm not hurt."

"I know what you said. Now are you going to do as I ask, or do I have to put you inside this vehicle myself?"

Julie could see it wouldn't do any good to argue; he was determined to do things his way. "Oh, all right," she said with a complete lack of graciousness.

He slipped into the driver's seat and exhaled slowly. "Thank you."

Julie crossed her arms and tried to stifle a laugh.

"What's so funny?"

"Nothing," but then she couldn't help it and burst out laughing.

"What?"

"It's you," she said between peals of laughter. "You said 'thank you.' Were you thanking me for sparing you the effort of having to physically lift me?"

"No." He apparently lacked even the most rudimentary sense of humor. "I was thanking you for not putting up any more of a fuss than you already have."

He started the engine. "What are you doing here, anyway?"

Until he asked, she'd completely forgotten. "Dad's lunch. It's on the bike. He forgot it this morning and I was taking it to him." She turned around and looked behind her, wondering if his lunch had somehow survived the collision. "I need to get it to him."

"Your father can go without lunch—getting you to a doctor is more important at the moment."

She glared at him, and he groaned audibly.

"Oh, all right." Without her having to say another word, he drove up to the main entrance and parked. "Stay right where you are," Fletcher warned.

"I wouldn't dream of doing anything else," she said with exaggerated sweetness.

He looked as though he doubted her, then quickly leaped out of the car. Removing her sorely bent and abused ten-speed, he leaned it against the building. She couldn't see what he was doing, but a moment later, the side mirror on the passenger door gave her a brief view of him on his cell phone.

"Did you tell my dad I wasn't hurt?" she asked when he got back in the car.

"No, I was talking to Dr. Wilbur."

Great, just great. Her father would find her bike, a crumpled mess, and assume the worst. "Give me that phone."

He stared at her as if no one ever spoke to him like that. "Please," she added, realizing how rude she must sound. "I've got to tell Dad I'm all right. He won't know what to think if he finds that."

"By the way," he said wryly, "his lunch did not sustain any mishap. The turkey sandwich isn't smashed at all. I thought you'd want to know." He reached inside his jacket and handed her the cell, which was the tiniest phone she'd ever seen. It took Julie a few minutes to figure out how it worked.

Her father was away from his desk and once again she had to leave a message with someone else. She explained the situation and added that he should collect his lunch from her bike.

"Are you happy now?" Fletcher asked when she'd finished and returned the cell.

"Ecstatic."

"Good. Now sit back and relax."

"Don't be so bossy," she muttered.

"Don't be so stubborn."

"This really isn't necessary. I have no intention of suing," she said, not for the first time.

"Good thing, because you'd lose."

Julie thought she saw a hint of a smile. She looked again, certain she must be wrong. The high-

and-mighty computer whiz was actually amused. Now *this* was something to write home about.

ANNE FLETCHER pulled the blanket around her shoulders as she attempted to fall to sleep. Opening one eye, she peered at the clock. Two in the morning. She should've been asleep hours ago. For no reason she could discern, she'd been having trouble sleeping. No matter what she did—read, drank warm milk, swallowed nighttime aspirin—she remained fully awake.

With a disgusted sigh, she tossed back the covers and reached for the switch on her lamp. She was wide awake and any effort to sleep would be a waste of time. Her mind drifted to the memory of the angel who'd appeared to her. She leaned over to get her sketchbook from the bedside table and flipped the pages until she found what she wanted.

Anne was sure she'd imagined the visitation, and yet it had seemed so real. But none of this made sense. Why would an angel appear to *her?* Not a word had been spoken, not a sound uttered. But an angel had stood directly in front of her. So strong was the impression that even now Anne could feel the love emanating from the heavenly being.

To further confuse her, the image had lasted for several minutes, long enough for Anne to grab her sketchbook. Almost as if she was posing, the angel had stood perfectly still while Anne quickly outlined what was before her, unbelievable though it was.

"She was so beautiful," Anne whispered as she studied the drawing with fresh eyes.

The urge to paint the image onto canvas suddenly gripped her. After a long day in her studio, she should be exhausted; instead, she was filled with excitement. Anne climbed out of bed. Dressed in her nightgown and slippers, she decided she'd paint until she felt tired. She'd get started and see how things went.

The studio was cold and dark, and she switched on the light, then hurried into the kitchen to make a pot of tea. Taking a pristine canvas from the pile stacked against the wall, she set it on the easel and stepped back. No, bigger. The angel who'd visited her couldn't be displayed on such a small space. Searching through her supplies, Anne looked for the largest canvas she had.

She found one in a closet, bigger than anything she'd ever used before, and began to work. Thinking she'd soon grow tired, she didn't pause. She painted through the night and didn't stop until daylight. To her amazement, she noticed sunshine pouring in around her. She glanced at the clock on the wall. Almost eight! For the first time in her life she'd worked straight through the night.

"I'll just take a quick break," she told herself as she went back to bed. Exhausted, she climbed between the sheets and closed her eyes. Seven hours later, around three, she woke feeling refreshed and revitalized.

After showering and changing clothes, Anne resumed her painting. The next time she looked up, it was dark again. Shocked, she realized she hadn't eaten in nearly thirty hours. The refrigerator provided a chunk of cheddar and a small cluster of seedless grapes, which she munched on hungrily. She made another pot of tea. Then it was back to work.

When she'd finished the painting, it was light again; for the second night in a row, she'd worked without sleep. Stepping back, Anne examined her creation with a critical eye.

"Yes," she whispered, awed by the painting before her.

This was her best work to date. She'd call it…*Visitation.* Smiling, she studied the painting from several angles.

The phone rang, startling her, and she hurried to answer it.

"Anne, it's Marta."

"Oh, Marta, hello." Her mind raced frantically as she tried to remember what day it was. Anne had a terrible feeling she'd missed their dinner appointment—not to mention her lunch with Roy—and sincerely hoped she hadn't. She thought for a minute; as far as she could calculate, it was Thursday morning now. Never had she worked on a project in such a frenzied fashion—to the point that she no longer knew what day of the week it was.

"I just called to ask if you'd let me see one of your paintings."

"Oh, Marta, are you sure?" Anne would never presume to ask her friend for this kind of favor.

"I've been hearing good things about your landscapes. A colleague of mine was on the island last summer—Kathy Gruber—and met you. She saw your work at a local exhibit. You remember her, don't you?"

"Yes, of course."

"Since I'm in town this week, I'd like to take a look at one of your pieces."

Anne glanced at her angel. "I'll let you see one, but it isn't a landscape. As it happens, I just finished it." Eyeing the canvas, she frowned. The painting was too big; she couldn't bring it into town with her. "It won't fit in my car," she murmured.

"I can make a trip out to your place tomorrow afternoon, if that's convenient."

"Of course it is, but we're still meeting for dinner, aren't we?"

"I wouldn't miss it for the world," Marta assured her.

"Me, neither," Anne said.

They spoke for a few minutes longer. When Anne replaced the receiver, she saw by the clock that she had just enough time for a short nap and a shower before heading into Seattle to meet her son.

CHAPTER SIX

"NOT BAD," Goodness said, staring at the painting. She cocked her head to one side and decided that, as a portrait, it was uncannily accurate. "It certainly looks like Shirley."

"I had no idea I was so lovely," Shirley said, clasping her hands. "Is that truly the way Anne sees me?" She looked expectantly at her two friends.

"So it seems," Goodness replied.

"What I want to know," Mercy began, making herself at home in Anne's studio, "is why we haven't been dragged back to Heaven in disgrace." She glanced pointedly at Shirley. "By all rights, we should be standing guard at the Pearly Gates after the stunt *she* pulled."

Mercy was the one more accustomed to causing trouble on Earth. It used to be Shirley who made them tread the straight and narrow, but it seemed the job had unfairly fallen to Goodness. For this assignment, anyway.

She couldn't give Mercy an answer. Apparently the Archangel had his own reasons for keeping them on Earth.

"We have an important task," Shirley explained

as if that should be obvious. ''Anne and Roy need us.''

''Seems to me Julie could use a hand, too,'' Goodness muttered. She didn't want to be judgmental, but the woman Mercy considered the answer to Anne's prayer was being less than cooperative.

''What do you mean?'' Mercy demanded. ''I thought the accident was a brilliant idea! It got Roy and Julie together, didn't it?''

''Yes, but all they did was snipe at each other.'' Goodness wasn't disparaging her friend's effort, but it simply hadn't worked.

''I think I was more optimistic than I should've been,'' Mercy said when Shirley came and sat next to her.

''I thought everything went very well,'' Shirley seemed undeterred by Julie's lack of cooperation—or Roy's. She continued to stare at her portrait with an appreciative eye.

''How can you say that?'' Goodness cried. In her opinion, Julie wasn't the only one who needed instruction in romance. Shirley obviously had difficulty recognizing what worked and what didn't. That staged accident certainly hadn't.

Shirley sighed. ''I had real hope when Roy offered to take her to his own physician.''

''But then he dumped her there.''

Mercy nodded vigorously. ''The least he could've done was wait long enough to make sure she wasn't injured.''

"He did pay for her taxi ride home," Shirley said. "They were getting along so well, too."

Goodness gaped at her friend and wondered if Shirley had lost touch with reality. "All they did was argue!" She'd witnessed courtroom battles with less antagonism. Roy Fletcher and Julie Wilcoff were completely unsuited as a couple, but no one wanted to listen to *her.* As far as she could see, the two of them didn't even like each other.

Goodness might never have been in love—romance was for earthly beings—but she had an instinct for matchmaking, if she did say so herself. She'd successfully guided men and women toward each other a time or two, but none of that seemed to matter.

"Yes, they were arguing, but I was well aware even if you weren't that they like each other," Mercy insisted.

"I don't think so." Goodness hated to discourage her friends, but she didn't see it. The spark just wasn't there. She suspected Julie had become so discouraged about her prospects of finding a husband that she'd lost the ability to attract one. Goodness had wanted to shake the young woman for joking about her weight. A lady never discussed such things! Julie should know better. And Roy—he was one of the walking wounded. He didn't seem capable of feeling anything, except bitterness and cynicism.

"What are you suggesting?" Mercy asked.

Goodness knew it was one thing to criticize and another to offer an alternative. But she figured they'd better face up to the truth sooner rather than later. ''We should give it up and search elsewhere.''

Mercy folded her wings tightly, a sure sign she wasn't pleased.

''We did our part. Now it's up to the two of them. Agreed?'' Goodness gave her friends a stern look.

''Just who do you think would interest Roy?'' Shirley asked.

''Just who?'' Mercy parroted.

They had Goodness there. ''I don't know—yet,'' she said. ''But we've done our part. Agreed?'' she said again.

The other two nodded with unmistakable reluctance.

''Now I say we leave them alone, and if it's meant to be, it'll happen without any help from the three of us.''

Mercy's mouth opened as if she was about to argue, but then she sighed loudly. ''Oh, all right, but I still have a strong feeling that Julie's the answer to Anne's prayer.''

''Anne,'' Shirley whispered. As if she'd suddenly remembered something, the former Guardian Angel announced, ''I'll be right back.''

Goodness was having none of this. ''Where are you going?''

Shirley glanced over her shoulder. ''I'll only be a minute.''

Goodness exchanged a look with Mercy and both followed Shirley. The other Ambassador didn't go far. She crept into Anne's bedroom and saw that the older woman was in bed, eyes closed.

"Is she asleep?" Mercy asked, floating above the bed.

"Not quite," Shirley answered with confidence.

Goodness peered closer, but couldn't tell. After working two consecutive nights on the portrait of Shirley, Anne must be exhausted.

"She's meeting her son later this morning," Mercy said. "She won't sleep long."

Goodness checked the clock radio. "The alarm is set."

"She thinks she only needs an hour or two."

"The poor thing," Shirley said. To Goodness's surprise, she moved to stand over the older woman. Gently pressing her hand to Anne's forehead, Shirley leaned forward to whisper, "You did a beautiful job." Then she lifted her hand and eased away.

"Look," Mercy said, pointing at Anne.

The softest of smiles touched the woman's lips, almost as if she'd heard Shirley speak.

"ROY?"

Roy glanced up at George Williams, his high-priced corporate attorney. "I'm sorry, did I miss something?" From the exasperated look on the other man's face, apparently he had. Williams had been discussing the profit-and-loss statement for Griffin

Plastics, a company Roy was interested in purchasing. He'd half heard Williams drone on about "synergies"—which, as far as he could determine, just meant that Griffin would be able to make the cases for his security software. Sighing, he directed his attention to the papers on his desk. "Let me look over these figures and get back to you later this afternoon."

The attorney frowned, gathered his files together and stuffed them into his briefcase.

"Before you leave I have a question," Roy said.

"About the Griffin figures?"

"No." Roy reached for a pen and made a few scribbles on a clean sheet of paper while he gathered his thoughts. "Late last week, I had a minor… altercation with a bicycle rider."

"Altercation?" George Williams repeated.

"She fell—" he chose the word carefully "—off her ten-speed and hit a tree."

The attorney's eyes widened and he pulled a blank pad of paper toward him.

"She was unhurt," Roy rushed to add. "As an innocent bystander, I immediately phoned the paramedics and notified the police."

"So, you're telling me that you were in no way responsible for her…fall?"

"That's correct."

"In other words, you happened along shortly after the accident, and out of consideration for this biker you stopped your vehicle and saw to her welfare?"

The attorney was describing a rather different scene than the one that had actually occurred, but Roy let him. "Yes," he said slowly, thoughtfully.

"Your concern is?" Williams asked.

"The woman claims I caused her accident." Just thinking about it irritated Roy. Although there was no evidence to validate her accusation, Julie Wilcoff had insisted he'd run into the rear of her bike. In fact, he didn't even see her until the last possible second and had instantly slammed on his brakes. In mentally reviewing the incident, Roy had decided that the sound of his car behind her must have startled Julie. At that point she'd lost focus and hit something in the road, which was the reason she'd catapulted off the bicycle and into the tree.

That, however, didn't explain the damage to her ten-speed. The bicycle clearly showed the impact from the rear. The back wheel was destroyed, the metal twisted and crumpled. Anyone looking at the bike would believe he'd hit Julie. But Roy knew otherwise, and there was no evidence on his car to suggest he'd collided with her.

"What injuries did she sustain?"

"None. She was unhurt. In fact, she refused medical treatment from the paramedics."

Williams frowned.

"I took her to my personal physician and he couldn't find any injuries, either."

The attorney scribbled furiously. "What have you heard from her since?"

"Nothing." That concerned him the most. With his name and his money, he was a natural target for frivolous lawsuits. However, any suit Julie filed might find a sympathetic jury. She could have a case, innocent though he was. It wasn't unheard of for a jury to award a huge settlement for a minor infraction, depending on how effectively the case was presented.

"I did feel bad," Roy said cautiously. "The accident occurred on company property and I did replace her bicycle." The new one was twice the machine her old ten-speed had been.

Again Williams made a notation. Roy worried that replacing Julie's ten-speed might be seen as an acknowledgment of guilt. He should've thought about that sooner.

"Did she have a reason for being on company property?" Williams asked.

"I employ her father."

The frown was back, creasing his brow. "I see."

"Wilcoff was only recently hired." Roy had let chance make the decision. He'd reviewed the applications, chosen the top three and written the candidates' names on slips of paper, which he'd placed in an empty coffee mug. He'd drawn one name—Dean's. So perhaps all of this was fated....

"Have you spoken to the father since the incident?"

Roy hadn't. "Any suggestions on what I should do now?"

"I wish you'd said something sooner," the attorney murmured, his expression darkening.

Roy probably should have, but until now he hadn't seen the need. It hadn't been a serious accident. By her own admission and confirmed by his doctor, Julie was perfectly fine. This sort of situation had never occurred until last Saturday. Williams was probably right; he should've consulted a lawyer earlier.

"Trouble?" he asked, unwilling to borrow any. He had problems enough.

Williams nodded abruptly. "Even if you haven't heard from this woman, that doesn't mean she isn't filing a lawsuit against you."

"She hasn't got a case," Roy argued. But she did have the damaged bicycle....

"You and I know that, but didn't you say she claims you were responsible for the accident?"

More times than Roy cared to count. Julie had repeatedly accused him of running her down. It had become her mantra on their ride to Dr. Wilbur's.

"That tells me there's a good possibility of a nuisance suit."

Roy should have known, should have guessed. "What do you think I should do next?" he asked, tension tightening his jaw. The thought of paying this money-grubber a dime was against his principles.

"Offer her a settlement."

He didn't want to do that, not in the least, but he

was wise enough to know it was better to take care of such unpleasantness quickly. Otherwise he might end up dealing with her in court. She had the damaged bike in her possession. A long, drawn-out trial would drain him emotionally and threaten him financially. And, needless to say, it could destroy his reputation.

"How much?" he asked bluntly.

The attorney hesitated, then said, "My expertise is corporate law, so perhaps it would be better to let a litigation expert answer that question."

Roy wasn't willing to waste another minute on this matter. "How much would *you* suggest?"

Williams shrugged. "Twenty-five thousand should more than compensate her for any pain and suffering."

As far as Roy was concerned, that was twenty-five thousand too much. But gritting his teeth, he agreed. He'd order the check cut right away.

"Anything else?" Williams asked, collecting his briefcase.

"No, that should be all."

The attorney gestured at the Griffin papers in front of Roy. "You'll get back to me this afternoon?"

Roy nodded. He'd read over the figures and make a decision by the end of the workday. He stood, and the two men shook hands. Williams saw himself out as Roy returned to his chair.

He leaned back and steepled his fingers, his mind spinning in unpleasant directions. Shaking his head, he picked up the Griffin file. Try as he might to focus on the facts and figures regarding the buyout, his thoughts wandered to Julie Wilcoff. Part of him wanted to take her at her word—to believe that she had no intention of suing him. But his experience with women said otherwise.

"You know by now you can't trust a woman." Until he heard the words, Roy didn't realize he'd spoken aloud.

Hoping to get a better feel for the situation, he called his executive assistant, Ms. Eleanor Johnson, and asked her to have Dean Wilcoff sent to his office immediately. This potential lawsuit would bother him until he had some sense of what was likely to happen. The best way to find that out was through Julie's father.

Within a matter of minutes, his new head of security was shown into his office.

"Good morning, Dean." The older man stood by his desk, shoulders squared in military fashion.

"Sit down." Roy motioned toward the chair recently vacated by his attorney. "I asked to see you on a personal matter."

The other man didn't react at all. That was good. "I imagine you heard about your daughter's bicycle accident."

Dean nodded. "She told me about it herself. I want you to know how much I appreciate the way you took care of her."

Roy dismissed his thanks. ''She received the new ten-speed?'' He'd had it delivered on Monday.

''She did, and I'm sure she'll want to thank you personally for your generosity.''

''That isn't necessary.'' Roy hesitated, uncertain how to phrase the next question. ''Uh, how is Julie?''

''How is she?'' the other man repeated as if he didn't understand. ''Oh, do you mean does she have any lingering aches and such from the fall?''

''Yes,'' Roy said without elaborating. He didn't want to tip Wilcoff off about his fear of a lawsuit. Sure as hell, Julie was talking to some fancy lawyer who'd promise her millions. Roy's millions. The tension gathered in his shoulder blades, tightening his muscles.

''Julie's tough,'' Dean answered, seeming to relax for the first time since entering the office. ''As a kid, she had more scraped knees and bruises than any boy in the neighborhood. I will admit that when I saw her bike, I was a bit concerned, but she's not showing any ill effects from the accident.''

''I'm glad to hear it.''

''Like I said, Julie's tough.''

''She's been able to work all week, then?'' That was another important question. If she was badly hurt, as she might later claim, her showing up at work would be evidence to suggest her claims were only an effort to bilk him out of as much money as possible.

"Oh, sure. She went to school every day this week."

This was sounding better all the time, but it was no guarantee that she wasn't planning legal action at some later point. No, it was best to deal with this once and for all.

"Your daughter's convinced I caused the collision." There, he'd said it. He watched the other man closely, wondering how he'd respond.

Wilcoff dropped his gaze. "Yes, she did mention that."

Aha! Roy knew it. This was exactly what Williams had warned him would happen. Not hearing from Julie didn't mean he wasn't being set up for a multimillion-dollar lawsuit.

"I feel bad about the accident," he said, carefully selecting his words. "While Julie and I have a disagreement as to the cause, I'd like to remind you she was riding on company grounds."

Wilcoff heard the censure in Roy's voice and reacted accordingly. "I'll make sure she doesn't do that again."

"I'd appreciate it." Another accident on his property was the last thing he needed.

"Consider it done," Wilcoff said. He seemed eager to leave. "Was that all, Mr. Fletcher?"

"Actually, no," Roy said slowly. This next part nearly stuck in his throat, but he had no option. "I'd like to offer Julie a small settlement to compensate for her pain and suffering."

Shocked, his head of security held up both hands. "That isn't necessary. In fact, I think Julie would be rather upset—"

"I insist. I'll have my attorney draw up the papers and we'll consider the matter closed."

Wilcoff shook his head. "None of this is necessary. Anyway, you should talk to Julie about it, not me. But I'm sure she'll feel the same way."

"Perhaps," Roy said, although he didn't believe it. He was a prime candidate for a lawsuit. He'd behaved stupidly in not getting his lawyer involved earlier. That oversight was a rarity for him; he hadn't come this far in the business world by ignoring the obvious.

"Whatever you decide, Mr. Fletcher, is between you and my daughter, but I'm certain Julie isn't interested in a settlement."

That's what they all say, Roy thought. Julie Wilcoff was no different from any other woman he'd met. Or any other man in the same situation, for that matter.

He was worried, but he didn't dare let it show.

Wilcoff left, and Roy started to read over the Griffin paperwork, but couldn't concentrate. The truth of it was, he'd quite enjoyed his exchanges with Julie Wilcoff. True, she wasn't the most attractive woman he'd ever known, but she possessed a quick wit and a quirky sense of humor. He couldn't recall the last time any woman had joked with him about her size or weight. He had to admit he found it refreshing.

His phone rang and he answered it. "I'm sorry to bother you, Mr. Fletcher," Eleanor Johnson said, "but your mother is here."

"My mother?" Oh, yes, now he remembered. In fact, he'd put it in his daily planner. She'd said something about meeting him for lunch on Thursday. In his current frame of mind, he had no interest in food, but he couldn't slight his mother. He sighed, then said with obvious reluctance, "Send her in."

"Merry Christmas, Roy." Disregarding his mood, his mother came into the office and hugged him.

"How are you, Mother? And isn't it a little early for Christmas greetings?"

"Not at all," she said, smiling at him with sparkling blue eyes. "Once December arrives, it's never too early to say Merry Christmas." Roy smiled in return. He sincerely loved his mother. She often frustrated him, but he did love and admire her—although he didn't understand her. She'd allowed his father to swindle her out of thousands. Roy had wanted her to fight, had urged her to drag his father back into court and make him pay. Roy wanted his father's reputation destroyed, which was what Burton Fletcher deserved, but his mother had refused to do it. His father seemed to have some regrets, if his efforts to contact Roy were any indication, but so far Roy had adamantly rejected any kind of relationship.

Instead of fighting, his mother had apparently forgiven Burton and become a hermit, living in a ridiculously small cottage on a tiny San Juan island. What really upset him was that she claimed to be happy. *Happy?* She'd been cheated, dumped and cast aside like yesterday's junk mail and she was happy? Roy just didn't get it.

"Are you ready for lunch?

Roy couldn't think of a way to tell her he didn't feel like having lunch without disappointing her. He checked his watch.

"Is your meeting over?"

"Yup, I have half an hour," he said. His problem was that he couldn't be around his mother and ignore the past. When he was with her, his heart ached for a life that was dead to him. He grieved for the innocents they'd once been, he and his mother. She'd taken one path since the divorce and he'd taken another. Hatred for his father and for Aimee consumed him. He wanted them to suffer, wanted them to rot in hell for all the pain they'd caused.

While his mother chose to forgive and forget, he chose to remember every detail, every incident, every minute of their treachery. In retrospect, he realized Aimee had been interested in his father all along. He'd never been anything more than the means to an end.

"I'll take whatever time you have for me," his mother said in the complacent voice that always perturbed him. "Oh," she said, slipping her arm around his waist. "I have a painting I want you to look at one day soon."

"Another landscape?" Without her knowledge, he'd purchased several of her pieces, under whatever name she used. Mary Something? He couldn't remember at the moment. She refused his financial help, but what she didn't know couldn't hurt her.

"Not this time," she said, then softly added, "This time I painted something entirely different."

CHAPTER SEVEN

"YOU DON'T KNOW how good it is to see you!" Marta Rosenberg greeted Anne, throwing her arms wide. The hotel foyer was dominated by a fifteen-foot-tall Christmas tree decorated with huge shiny red balls and large gold bows. Plush leather chairs and mahogany tables created an intimate atmosphere despite the openness of the room.

Anne hugged her friend. It'd been years since they'd last visited. Nearly ten if she remembered correctly. Burton had taken a business trip to New York and Anne had accompanied him. They'd gone to a show on Broadway, visited old friends and strolled leisurely through Central Park holding hands. She and Marta had met for drinks one afternoon, gossiping and laughing like the college girls they'd once been. That was long before Aimee, long before the divorce.

A familiar ache stabbed Anne close to her heart. She made an effort to ignore it; she wouldn't allow her loss to taint this reunion.

"You look marvelous," Marta said, stepping back to get a better view. "What have you been up to?"

Anne laughed off her old friend's praise. ''I spent most of the afternoon buying Christmas cards and wrap—after I had lunch with Roy. I swear Scrooge has more Christmas spirit than my son.'' Her elegant white suit was left over from her old life. These days, she was most comfortable in jeans and an oil-smeared cotton shirt.

Marta was blond and tanned and she dressed strictly in black, no matter what the season. It was a New York thing, Anne figured. Her friend's hair haphazardly framed her face, but Anne knew there was nothing haphazard about it. She looked chic, rich, sophisticated, and her world seemed a million miles from the one that had become Anne's.

''Speaking of Roy,'' Marta said as she led the way into the dining room. ''I understand he's making quite a name for himself.''

''I'm very proud of what he's accomplished, but I worry about him.'' She didn't elaborate and thankfully Marta didn't question her. Despite her determination to enjoy this evening, Anne's thoughts went back to the lunch with Roy. He seemed preoccupied, but when she'd asked him about it, he'd brushed aside her concern. He so rarely allowed her glimpses into his life; he'd closed himself off from her, the same way he'd shut out everyone else.

Marta announced her name to the maître d', and they were immediately seated. The man handed Anne a leather-encased menu, and with more ceremony than necessary, draped the white linen napkin on her lap.

A waiter came for their drink order, and both Anne and Marta requested a glass of white wine.

"What brings you to Seattle?" Anne asked her. "Business, I assume."

"What else? At one time I had a life, but now it's art. You wouldn't believe some of the pieces I've found. And, before you dismiss my interest, I really would like to see your work."

"I've only been painting for the last five years, Marta. My work is amateurish compared to the artists you represent."

"Let me decide that. You were the most talented girl in our class and I don't expect that's changed."

But it had. So much had changed in the forty years since Marta had first known her.

Their wine arrived, and they paused to sample it. Anne welcomed the break in conversation.

"Well," Marta said as she set her wineglass aside. "Let's get the subject of Burton out of the way. What happened?"

Anne gazed sightlessly into the distance. "What always happens?"

"Another woman." Marta scowled as she added, "Younger, no doubt."

Anne nodded. "Thirty years younger."

"I hope he paid through the nose for this."

Anne didn't answer. How could she? "Actually, no." The details weren't anyone's business but her own. "It depresses me to discuss it, so let's not, all right?"

"The jerk," Marta muttered, and said something else under her breath, something Anne wouldn't ask her to repeat.

"Shall we make a toast to independence?" Marta asked, tears filling her eyes.

"Marta?" Anne leaned forward and touched her friend's hand. "What's wrong?"

"What's always wrong?" she murmured, echoing Anne's earlier statement.

"Jack?"

Marta nodded, lowering her eyes. "He's got a girlfriend. Naturally, he doesn't think I know, but a blind woman could've figured it out."

So this was the reason Marta had sought her out. "What are you going to do?"

"Twenty-seven years with a man, and you think you know him. Silly me." She made a gallant effort to smile through her tears. Raising the wineglass to her lips, she took a long and appreciative swallow.

"You're considering a divorce?"

Marta shrugged. "I don't know yet. I can't imagine the rest of my life without Jack, but I can't tolerate the thought of him with another woman—especially while he's married to me! I don't know what to do."

Anne noticed that her friend's hand trembled as she put down her wineglass. "Half the time I want to bash his head in for hurting me like this and the rest of the time I cry."

"You're sure he's having an affair?"

Marta reached for her wine and took another large swallow. "Very sure." Tears glistened in her eyes again. "All right, my wise friend, advise me."

Anne felt in no position to be giving her advice, although she supposed she could tell Marta what *not* to do. She'd been cheated and misled, and all because she'd been naive. The waiter appeared at their table, and Anne realized they hadn't even looked at their menus. They did so quickly, both deciding on the salmon entrée, and made their selections.

Resuming the conversation, Anne called on her own experience. The first thing she suggested was that Marta talk to an attorney, and not one her husband recommended. From this point forward, everything Jack said was suspect, since he'd lied to her already. Marta needed facts and information. Anne might have saved herself a lot of grief had she hired an attorney of her own choosing—and done so earlier.

Their dinners arrived. They chatted, they ate, they laughed and cried, and then laughed again.

"I can't tell you how wonderful it is to talk with someone openly and honestly," Marta said after their second glass of wine and two cups of strong coffee. "I didn't know where else to turn. Lots of our friends have split up over the years, but…this just can't be happening. Not to me and Jack, and yet it is, and I don't know what to do about it.''

Anne squeezed Marta's hand. ''I so hoped Burton would come to his senses. I prayed and pleaded with God to give me my husband back. My entire identity was tied up with his.''

Marta's eyes filled again. ''I'm beginning to wonder if God answers our prayers.''

Anne believed He did. ''While it's true God didn't give me the answer I *wanted,* He did answer me.''

''How do you mean?''

''I have my own identity now, and it isn't that of Burton's ex-wife. I'm Anne Fletcher—and I'm also Mary Flemming, artist.''

''Why did you decide to use a pseudonym?''

It was a well-kept secret. Only a few people knew. Her fear was that friends, out of pity and concern, would purchase her landscapes in an effort to support her. Anne didn't want their sympathy. Come hell or high water, she was determined to make it on her own.

''Mary Flemming is business-savvy, smart and talented. Anne Fletcher is meek, mild and a victim, as far as the world's concerned.''

''I love it,'' Marta said, reaching for the tab and signing it to her room. ''Speaking of Mary,'' she said, looking up, ''I'm really looking forward to seeing her work.''

Anne hesitated. ''You're sure about this?''

"Is that Anne or Mary speaking?"

"Anne," she confessed with a laugh.

"That's what I thought."

"Okay, come to my car with me. I brought a sketch."

They left the hotel, and Anne handed the valet her claim check. He quickly brought her car around, and at Anne's instructions, parked it at the outside curb to avoid delaying anyone pulling into the portico. The Cadillac was one of the few things she'd gotten as part of the divorce settlement. Roy said that was because Burton had wanted it to look as if he'd been fair.

"As I explained, this isn't one of my landscapes," Anne said, opening the door. Because of the size of the painting, she'd brought along her sketchbook. It lay on the passenger seat, and Anne picked it up and opened it to the sketch of the angel.

For a long moment Marta didn't say anything. "This is the sketch you painted from?"

"Yes, in a huge rush." She told her the size of the canvas. While on the ferry, she'd shaded in the sketch, using pencils. "Like I said this morning, I just finished the painting. I'm sure the oil is still wet." Then, because she regretted showing her art to such a renowned professional, Anne quickly added, "Listen, it's all right if you don't like it."

"Like it?" Marta said, meeting her gaze. "I *love* it. This is incredible. I realize it's only a sketch, but if the painting is anything like this, you have a real winner on your hands. Maybe it's my state of mind, I don't know," she said, staring down at the pad, "but I feel like...like I've been touched by God just looking at it."

Anne could hardly believe Marta had said that....

"I'm stopping by your place first thing tomorrow morning, and if this painting is half as good as I think it'll be, I'm taking it back to New York. Agreed?"

"I...of course."

"I can get eight or nine for this."

"Hundred?"

Marta grinned. "Thousand."

"Eight or nine thousand?" Anne was sure she was dreaming now.

"Maybe more."

Anne wanted to throw her arms in the air and scream for joy. Instead, she clasped both hands over her mouth and silently said a prayer of gratitude.

CHAPTER EIGHT

NOW THAT HER FATHER was working, Julie always stopped at the mailbox on her way home from school. She sorted through the daily offering of bills, notices, an occasional letter and a plethora of the usual junk mail. As she strolled toward the house on Monday, she shuffled through the day's collection and paused at the thick manila envelope addressed to her. Julie hesitated in midstep. The return address was that of a well-known Seattle law firm.

Tearing it open, Julie juggled the house keys, the rest of the mail and her backpack as she extracted a letter and a thick wad of paper. Using her shoulder to open the door, she nearly fell into the house when she realized what she was reading.

A settlement offer.

From Roy Fletcher.

Julie scanned the details and by the time she'd finished she could hardly breathe. Mr. High-and-Mighty wanted to buy her off. He was willing to spend twenty-five thousand dollars to shut her up. Julie couldn't believe it, couldn't comprehend why anyone would go to such outlandish lengths to get rid of her, especially when she'd assured him she had no intention of suing.

She didn't want his money. She didn't want anything from him. His offer was the biggest insult of her life.

Pacing now, she stomped from one end of the living room to the other. She knew it wasn't a good idea to try to reason with Fletcher, especially when she felt like this, but she couldn't stand still and she couldn't stay home. She had to do *something* before she exploded with indignation. This pent-up energy had to go somewhere.

Her thoughts continued to churn as she tossed her car keys in the air and deftly caught them. Good idea or not, her mind was made up. She was going to tell Mr. Big Bucks exactly what he could do with his "settlement offer."

Julie was so angry she barely noticed the ten-mile drive in heavy traffic. Naturally there wasn't a single parking space available anywhere at Fletcher Industries. With no other option open to her, she pulled into a handicapped spot.

Arms swinging at her sides, every step filled with determination, Julie headed for the company's headquarters. In the back of her mind a small voice whispered that this was probably a mistake. She didn't care. She was beyond caring.

She stormed into the building, past the security guard, a young man with impressive biceps. Jason, she recalled. She'd met him last week. "Miss," he said, stopping her. "You have to check in here first."

Julie waved her hand at him as he moved out from behind his desk. "You don't want to mess with me just now."

"Ma'am, I'm sorry, but I can't let you onto the elevator until you've been cleared by security."

"Hey, man, that's Mr. Wilcoff's daughter," a second guard said, coming around the corner. "How you doing?" he asked, as if they were the best of friends.

Julie vaguely remembered him from the day of her accident. Roy Fletcher had spoken to him briefly when he dropped off her bike at the office complex.

Julie smiled at the first guard, as if they were indeed well acquainted. "You remember me, don't you, Jason?" she said. "I came here with my dad about a week ago. How's it going?"

"All right, I guess," he said, eyeing her skeptically.

For once Julie was grateful for the family resemblance.

"I remember you now," he said after a moment. "Do you have an appointment with your father?"

Julie smiled—and lied through her teeth. She had an appointment, all right, an appointment with justice. "I do. I apologize if I was rude earlier."

"No problem." Eager to please his boss, the guard returned to his desk and reached for his phone. "I'll let your father know you're coming."

"Thanks," Julie said, and swallowed down a plea not to call him, after all. She stopped briefly at the company directory to find the location of Fletcher's office. Just as she'd suspected—top floor. Rushing, she pressed the elevator button and glanced at her watch, trying to gauge how much time she had before she was found out. Once her father knew she was in the building, he'd wonder where she was—and what she was doing.

At the top floor she stepped out of the elevator and faced a large desk. An efficient-looking middle-aged woman glanced up, her expression surprised.

"May I help you?" she asked politely.

"I'm here to see Mr. Fletcher."

"Do you have an appointment?"

This paragon who guarded the lion's den knew exactly when Fletcher had appointments scheduled, and Julie wasn't on any list.

"Oh, yes," she muttered, and without wasting another second, Julie bolted for the huge floor-to-ceiling double doors. Without bothering to knock, she turned the knob and barreled inside.

Fletcher was on the phone. Startled, he looked up. His gaze boldly met hers and he didn't so much as blink. She gave him credit for that. Tall as she was, *angry* as she was, Julie knew she made an intimidating sight.

"I'll need to phone you back," Fletcher said smoothly. "My office has just been invaded and I have a feeling this is going to take longer than you'll want to wait."

"Mr. Fletcher, I'm sorry, she just...came in." Ms. Johnson arrived seconds after Julie. The older woman was clearly flustered; presumably nothing like this had ever happened before. "I've contacted security—they're on their way up."

"Good plan." Fletcher slowly rose from his seat, leaning forward on his desk, his eyes never leaving Julie.

"Should I stay with you?" his assistant asked nervously.

"I'll be fine, Ms. Johnson."

"I wouldn't count on that," Julie muttered.

Fletcher waved his assistant out of the room and returned his attention to Julie. "You had something you wanted to say?"

"Your settlement offer arrived!" she cried. "Why would you do such a thing?"

"Why?" He cocked one brow as if to suggest it should be obvious.

"I told you I wasn't going to sue!"

He snickered.

"Are you so cynical that you don't trust *anyone?* So cynical you think you can buy your way out of everything?"

"Money is the universal language."

Julie folded her arms. "Listen to me, Fletcher, and listen hard. I don't want your money." She spoke slowly and emphatically so that even a man as emotionally obtuse as this one would get the point.

He angled his head sideways and stared at the ceiling. ''Where have I heard that before?'' Then, as if he was bored and ready to end the discussion, he said, ''You want the money. Everyone wants the money. Just sign the agreement and cash the check. You can be outraged all over again—and twenty-five thousand dollars richer.''

Julie's mouth sagged open. ''You don't get it, do you. I'm not cashing the check. I'm not signing the settlement.''

''Of course you're not signing the settlement,'' he snapped, his eyes so cold that for an instant she actually shivered.

She caught her breath and stepped back. ''It isn't just me you distrust,'' she whispered. He wasn't capable of trusting a single, solitary person. Some elemental betrayal had waylaid him in the past, and he'd never recovered, never moved beyond it. She didn't know what had happened; in fact, she didn't want to know. But right now they were at an impasse unless she could think of some way to settle this, some way that suited them both.

''All right,'' Julie said, thinking on her feet. ''Tell you what I'll do.''

''Ah, the bargaining begins. Are you sure you don't want your attorney here?''

''I don't have an attorney. Now listen, because I'm only going to say this once.''

"The schoolteacher speaks." He'd folded his arms and she relaxed hers.

"I'll sign your stupid agreement."

He flashed her a knowing, sarcastic grin. "I thought you'd come to your senses sooner or later."

"With one stipulation."

His smile vanished.

"I want a signed statement from you in which you concede that you caused the accident and—" she wagged her finger at his Cross pen "—I'd like a written apology."

His eyes narrowed and, if possible, grew even colder. Hands pressed on the top of his desk, he leaned forward again. "I didn't cause the accident and I'm damned if I'll apologize for something I didn't do."

She'd figured that would make him mad. Good. Maybe he'd understand how *she* felt. "Explain the damage to my bike, then," she said, forcing her voice to remain calm.

His lips thinned. "I can't."

"What does it matter? You get what you want and I get what I want."

"What *exactly* do you want?" he demanded.

"I already told you. And I already stated that I was only saying it once."

"Good luck, sister, because you're not getting any apology from me."

"Okay," she said cheerfully, and then because

she enjoyed riling him, she added, "Shall I have my attorney call yours?"

"I thought you didn't have an attorney," he challenged as if he'd welcome the opportunity to call her a bold-faced liar.

"I don't, at least not yet, but I imagine I won't have any problem finding one who'd be willing to take you to court."

"Julie..." Her father rushed into the room and stopped midway between Julie and Fletcher's desk. He spread his arms between the two of them, trying to assess the situation.

He looked at his boss first. "Mr. Fletcher, I apologize that my daughter burst into your office like that."

"Dad, you'd better hear me out before you apologize to that man." She gestured wildly at Fletcher. "He tried to buy me off with a settlement offer!"

"I know, honey."

"You know?"

Her father nodded. "Mr. Fletcher told me it was in the works, but it's none of my affair, so I didn't say anything."

"You involved my father in this?" Julie hissed at Fletcher.

"Sweetheart," her father said in the gentlest of tones, "perhaps it would be best if you left now."

"Not yet." Julie was determined to stand her ground. As far as she was concerned, this conversation was a long way from over.

Her father glanced apologetically at his employer. ''I'm afraid Julie's got a temper, sir.''

''Dad!''

''She takes after her mother in that.''

Julie was horrified to hear her father saying such a thing to a man who'd insulted her.

''I'm sorry, Jules,'' her father continued, ''but you don't leave me any other choice.'' That said, he attempted to hoist her fireman-style over his shoulder and forcibly remove her from the office. Julie didn't try to fight him, but she was far too heavy for him to carry. He did manage to lift her several inches off the ground.

''Dad! Put me down this instant.''

Either she weighed more than he'd assumed or he was willing to listen, because he set her down on the carpet.

''Thank you,'' she whispered.

''Julie, get out of this office,'' he said in a low, irate voice. ''*Now.*''

She could only imagine how amused Fletcher must be. ''Not until this is settled,'' she said, glaring at her father's employer.

Suddenly her father walked behind her and wrapped his arms around her waist. The shock of it caught her unawares and she toppled back against him. Satisfied, he started to drag her out of the room, the heels of her shoes making tracks in the plush carpeting.

''Let me go!'' she cried. When she looked up,

she saw Roy Fletcher grinning widely. "Don't you *dare* laugh," she warned, stretching out her arm and pointing at him.

"Bye-bye, Ms. Wilcoff." He waved and had the audacity to laugh outright.

Pulling out her hair seemed like the only viable option just then. "We aren't finished!" she shouted. "Daddy, for the love of heaven, release me."

"Not until we're in the elevator," her father said. He dragged her through the large double doors.

Fletcher walked around his desk and headed for the door. Julie wanted it understood that he hadn't heard the last of her. "Furthermore, you owe me an apology!"

Fletcher's assistant stood at her desk, eyes twinkling. "Nice to have met you, Ms. Wilcoff."

"You, too," Julie said, smiling weakly.

The elevator arrived. "This is your last chance, Fletcher!" she shouted.

"No, Julie," her father said as he entered the elevator car. The doors slid closed. "This is *your* last chance. I don't want you ever pulling a stunt like this again. Is that clear?"

She nodded. It was ridiculous to be chastised by her father at the age of thirty, but at the moment she felt more like twelve.

It seemed to take two lifetimes for the elevator car to descend to the lobby. The silence was so tense it almost crackled—like static electricity. One glance at her father, who was the calmest man she'd ever known, told her he was furious.

''You will apologize,'' he said just before the doors slid open.

She'd need to think about that for a moment.

''Your car's being towed,'' he announced without inflection. ''You took a handicapped parking space and you know better.''

She resisted stamping her foot. Yes, she did know better.

''You can either wait for me to get off work to drive you home or you can take the bus. There's one every half hour.''

Staying on Fletcher Industries property one second longer was intolerable. ''I'd rather walk,'' she muttered. It would help her work off some of her anger.

''I thought you might decide that.''

''He's an unreasonable man, Dad.''

Her father didn't answer. ''Jason,'' he said to the guard who'd first questioned her. ''Until you hear otherwise, my daughter is banned from the building.''

Jason placed his hand on his weapon, as if to suggest she'd better not enter this lobby again, not on his watch. ''Yes, sir!''

Great. Just great. If her father had anything to say about it, the next time she set foot on Fletcher property she'd likely be shot on sight.

CHAPTER NINE

ROY SAT BACK DOWN at his desk and for the first time in months—years—he burst out laughing. He laughed without restraint. Then he returned to work, stared at his computer screen, and started to laugh all over again.

The phone rang and Ms. Johnson interrupted his laughfest. ''Your mother's on line one.''

His mother? Not until Roy reached for the receiver did he recall that he'd just seen her the week before. He generally heard from her once a month; any more often was unusual. She'd said something about wanting him to see one of her paintings, but he'd told her he'd do that Christmas Day.

He picked up the receiver. ''Hello, Mom.''

The line was silent.

''Mom?''

''Roy, is that you? You don't sound like yourself.''

''It's me,'' he said. ''What's up?''

''Are you...'' She paused as if searching for the right word. ''You're not laughing, are you?''

''Laughing?'' he repeated, trying to sober his voice. ''I was earlier.''

''A joke?'' she asked.

''Actually, it was a woman. Her father's employed here and she stormed into my office filled with righteous indignation about some nonsense or other. I have to tell you, I don't think I've ever seen anything funnier.'' Humor overtook him again and he burst into waves of laughter as he described Julie's outrage. Soon his mother was laughing, too. She seemed to find the scene as hilarious as he did.

''What can I do for you?'' Roy asked as he wiped the mirth from his eyes.

''I wanted to make arrangements to come and paint,'' she said.

''I thought you wanted me to come to your house—to look at one of your paintings.''

She had him completely confused now. Did his mother actually believe he was going to let her do custodial work? ''What do you want to paint?''

''The lobby windows,'' she said as if it should be perfectly obvious. ''Remember? We talked about this a couple of weeks ago. I'm going to paint a holiday scene on the lobby windows.''

As far as Roy was concerned, Christmas wasn't all that different from any other day of the year. He'd do his duty and spend it with his mother; they'd exchange gifts against a background of decorations that brought back painful memories for him—painful because they were good. The truth was he no longer cared much for Christmas. The holidays didn't even resemble what he'd once known, those warm, happy times, joking with his parents, feeling their love for him and for each other. That had been a façade, he now realized. His father had grown cynical and jaded as the years passed. Roy hadn't seen that until it was too late. Far too late.

"Now that you've reminded me, I do remember. You can paint whatever you want, Mother," he told her. "I've already let the security people know."

"I have a wonderful idea."

She started to detail her plans—something about angels—but he cut her off. "Mother, this isn't the Sistine Chapel. Don't worry about it."

"I know, but…well, I was thinking I'd paint a religious scene with angels similar to the one in this painting I was telling you about. You wouldn't mind that, would you?"

There was no point in arguing with her even if he did object. "All right, paint your angels. I'll have the windows cleaned."

Her appreciative sigh came over the telephone line. "Thank you, Roy. I'll be there Wednesday."

"Fine."

"I'm not going to bother you," she assured him. "You won't even know I'm there."

This seemed to be his day for dealing with irrational women. He could hear the determination in his mother's voice. For whatever reason, she felt it was important to paint a Christmas scene, and not just any scene, either. But if painting angels on his windows made her happy, then he guessed there wasn't any harm in it.

"Fine, Mother, come and do as you wish."

"I promise you're going to love my Christmas angels."

Roy rolled his eyes. "I'm sure I will, Mother."

She seemed to be in a chatty mood and went on about dinner with her college friend. "I'm not keeping you from anything, am I?" she asked after talking nonstop for several minutes. "I know how busy you are."

For the first time in a very long while, Roy found he actually liked speaking to his mother—as much as he was capable of liking anything other than business. "It's fine, Mom."

For some reason, she seemed to get choked up over that and quickly ended the conversation. He replaced the receiver and stared down at the telephone, hardly knowing what to make of his mother. Women. He'd never understand them.

Roy worked for another half hour and then decided he wasn't in the mood. He wasn't sure *what* he wanted to do, but he was leaving the office. Any file he needed could be accessed from the computer at his condo—a sprawling five-thousand-square-foot penthouse suite overlooking Lake Washington.

As Roy left the elevator and walked into the lobby, he saw a truck towing a vehicle away from the handicapped parking slot. The car looked vaguely familiar.

Jason, the security guard, wore a satisfied grin. "Ms. Wilcoff's car," he said, answering Roy's unspoken question. "In her rush to get in to see you, she parked illegally. Her father wasn't willing to make allowances."

This was getting better all the time. "Where is she?"

"Her father said she could either take the bus or wait until he was available to give her a ride. She decided to walk."

That was exactly what Roy would have expected. "Any idea how much of a hike that is?" he asked.

Jason nodded. Grinning, he glanced down at the polished marble floor. "I think it's about ten miles."

A smile tempted Roy. "I see."

"You can rest assured she won't make it past me a second time, Mr. Fletcher. Her father's banned her from the building, too, so you don't have anything to worry about."

"I appreciate that," Roy said, pushing through the glass doors, but as he walked out of the building, he realized that wasn't true. He'd enjoyed his encounter with Julie, reveled in it. He felt alive in ways he'd forgotten.

Roy turned back. "Do you know which direction she was headed?" he asked the guard.

Jason looked surprised. "North, I'd guess."

"Thanks." Roy was going south himself, but a small detour wouldn't be amiss. He didn't think she'd accept his offer of a ride, but he'd ask. Perhaps a brisk walk would help her vent her anger and make her a little more amenable to reaching some kind of agreement.

Roy drove a black Lincoln Continental with tinted glass. He could see out but no one could see in, which was precisely the way he wanted it. He exited onto the main street heading north and stayed in the right-hand lane. He drove a couple of miles, mildly impressed by how far she'd gotten. She'd made good time. Perhaps she'd grown tired and taken a bus. Or perhaps she'd hailed a taxi.

Then he saw her, walking at a quick pace, arms swinging at her sides. Roy reduced his speed to a crawl as he approached her. Traffic wove around him, some cars honking with irritation, but he ignored them and pulled up alongside Julie. With the touch of a button, the passenger-side window glided down.

She glanced in his direction and her eyes widened when she recognized him.

"Get in," he said.

"Why should I?"

Time to play nice, he decided. "Please."

She hesitated, then walked to the curb and leaned down to talk to him. "Give me one reason I should do anything you say."

"I'll drive you home."

That didn't appear to influence her. "I'm halfway there already."

Horns blared behind him. "If you don't hurry up and decide, I'll get a traffic ticket."

"Good. It's what you deserve."

"Julie, come on, be reasonable. I said please."

She looked away and then capitulated. "Oh, all right."

She certainly wasn't gracious about it, but he felt thankful that she opened the passenger door without further ado and slid into the car. As he hit the gas, she fastened her seat belt.

"Give me your address," he said.

Obediently she rattled off the street and house number.

Now that she was in the car, Roy couldn't think of the right conversational gambit. He had no intention of meeting her demands and she apparently wasn't interested in complying with his. Silly woman. With the stroke of a pen, she could be twenty-five thousand dollars richer, but she was too stubborn to do it. Perhaps she was looking for more.

"You don't have anything to say?" she asked him after a moment.

"Nope. What about you?"

"Not a thing," she returned testily.

He eased off the main thoroughfare and onto a quiet side street. It was a middle-class neighborhood of older homes, mostly small ramblers with a few brick houses interspersed among them, just enough to keep the neighborhood from being termed a development.

"Are you ready to listen to reason yet?" he asked as if he possessed limitless patience and was more than willing to wait her out.

"Are you ready to accept responsibility and write me an apology?"

He didn't hesitate. "Not on your life."

"I'm not signing that settlement offer, either," she said, tossing him a saccharine smile. She exhaled sharply. "You can rest easy about one matter, however."

He looked away from the road to glance at her.

"I can't afford an attorney."

Far be it for Roy to point out that in liability cases lawyers were more than happy to accept a chunk of the settlement. Generally it was a big chunk. "Sorry to hear that."

"Yeah, I'll just bet you are."

She closed her eyes and leaned back.

Roy didn't completely understand why, but he found himself not wanting to drop her off at her house; he wanted to continue driving so they could talk. "We should discuss it further. Perhaps we could reach a compromise."

"Like what? I take twelve thousand five hundred dollars and you just apologize and not accept responsibility?"

"Something like that. Why don't we have coffee and talk it over?"

Julie's head snapped up. "You're joking, right? Did I just hear you invite me to coffee?"

"A gesture of peace and goodwill," he said in a conciliatory tone. "I hear this is the season for it."

"Oh puh-leeze." She crossed her arms. "Thanks but no thanks."

Roy shrugged off her rejection, although he had to admit he was disappointed. "I was only trying to be helpful."

"Were you?" Her eyes narrowed with suspicion.

"It's no big deal."

"You're sincere?"

"Yes," he said simply. He felt her scrutiny as he drove.

"All right," she muttered, "but I'd like to suggest we have coffee at my house."

Roy eased to a stop in front of the address she'd given him. It was a small, well-kept house, probably just two bedrooms. Green shutters bordered the windows and a rocking chair sat on the front porch. Christmas lights were strung along the roofline.

"You have coffee on?" he asked.

"No, but I'll make a pot."

"Why not a restaurant? Neutral territory."

"Because," she said, and sighed heavily. "I'd feel more comfortable on home turf."

He considered that. "Should I worry about being poisoned?"

"Hmm." A smile teased the edges of her mouth. "That's an interesting thought."

"Perhaps we can use this as a lesson in compromise," he suggested.

"Compromise? How do you mean?"

"If I come onto your turf, we'll order dinner and I'll buy—"

Julie didn't allow him to finish. "Dinner? I thought we were having coffee."

"I'm hungry," he said. "And we'll eat in the security and comfort of your home."

For a moment he thought she was about to reject that idea; then she turned to him and offered a tentative smile. "All right. We'll order pizza and I like anchovies."

"Pizza it is. I like anchovies, too." He'd never met a woman who did; once again she'd surprised him.

From the expression on her face, he wasn't sure she believed him.

"I'm just a regular guy, Julie."

Muttering, "That's what Benedict Arnold used to say," she climbed out of the car and closed the door.

Roy joined her on the concrete walkway that led to the front steps. "I'm really not so bad, you know."

"That remains to be seen, doesn't it?"

He chuckled. "I guess it does. Friends?" He held out his hand.

She looked at his extended hand, sighed and gave him her own. "Don't think this means I'm going to change my mind about the settlement check."

"We'll see about that," he said as she inserted the key into the lock.

"Yes, we will," she returned with equal determination.

Roy grinned. This might not be so bad. A girl who liked anchovies on her pizza was obviously reasonable *some* of the time.

CHAPTER TEN

EXHAUSTED, MERCY FLUNG herself onto a passing cloud. ''This romance business is hard work,'' she complained.

''But Julie's having dinner with him.'' For her part, Goodness felt encouraged. She had to give Dean Wilcoff's daughter credit; Julie had spunk, which was something Goodness admired.

The young woman hadn't been willing to accept Roy's settlement because money wasn't important to her. That was a rare human trait. The issue of earthly wealth confused Goodness. Money couldn't buy the things that were truly important. Roy owned a fabulous condo on prime waterfront real estate. The three of them had gone to it and investigated, needing to learn what they could about him. Goodness had hardly ever visited a more beautifully decorated place, but it wasn't a home. By the same token, Roy was surrounded by all kinds of people, employees and yes-men, but he had few friends. Those he'd once considered friends had drifted away out of neglect. While Roy was considered rich, he was one of the poorest humans Goodness had ever seen.

"He likes Julie," Shirley said with a rather smug smile.

"She amuses him." Goodness wasn't fooled. Roy had no real feelings for Julie. She wasn't typical of the women he'd known and he wasn't quite sure what to make of her. The laughter had been good for him. It had *felt* good, too, and that feeling had left him with the urge to laugh more. She suspected it was the reason he'd sought Julie out. Their shared pizza dinner had come about unexpectedly, and yet he was enjoying himself. They both were.

"Her stubborniness intrigues him," Goodness added. "He can't understand why she isn't interested in the settlement."

"Julie has principles," Shirley announced, "and Roy hasn't seen that in a woman in quite a while. Since before Aimee."

Mercy agreed. "What should happen next?"

The other angels looked at Goodness as if she was the one with the answers. "How should I know?" She shrugged, as much at a loss as her friends. This entire relationship was a fly-by-the-seat-of-your-pants affair. "I'm making this up as we go along."

"Yes, but you've done such good work so far."

"Me?" Goodness cried. "This is a team effort." She peered down through the cloud cover and stared into the house below. "They're eating their pizza now."

"And talking," Mercy noted with delight.

"No one seems to be yelling, either," Shirley said. "That's a good sign, don't you think?"

Goodness nodded. "He should ask her out next," she told the others, suddenly inspired. That seemed to be the most logical step. *Not* that she was convinced this relationship had much of a future.

"Out?" Mercy repeated. "You mean like on a date?"

"Yes, a date. He implied that he was interested in getting her on neutral turf, remember?" That was the way humans generally did those things, Goodness reasoned, because then no one had an unfair advantage. She gave a rueful grin. Humans tended to be so competitive....

"Roy doesn't date!" Mercy cried. "Not in years. He's forgotten how. Besides, he's got this thing about women." From the exasperated look she wore, one might think Goodness had suggested Roy propose marriage as his next move.

"Then he has to believe it *isn't* a date." Goodness's head was spinning. Surely there was some social event he was obliged to attend. December was the month for that sort of function.

"Think," Mercy demanded, as if this was a matter of life and death.

Suddenly the air brightened and with a sound like thunder the Archangel Gabriel joined them. He held a massive volume in his hands. *The Book of Lives.* "How's it going, ladies?" he inquired.

Goodness noticed that the three of them rushed to

give him brief updates. ‘‘Great,’’ she said cheerfully.

‘‘Yes—very good,’’ Mercy seconded.

‘‘We think Julie Wilcoff is the answer to Anne’s prayer,’’ Shirley told him. ‘‘They’re together now.’’

Gabriel looked impressed. ‘‘And you three arranged that?’’

Goodness swallowed hard. If she admitted their role in the bike accident, it could mean trouble. Much better if Gabriel didn’t know about their little scheme. ‘‘Not entirely,’’ she said—which was the truth. Still, it sounded becomingly modest.

‘‘How’s Anne?’’ Gabriel surprised her by asking.

Shirley, Goodness and Mercy froze. If he found out that Shirley had appeared to Anne, they could forget ever coming to Earth again. ‘‘Fine,’’ Goodness said, and to her horror her voice squeaked. ‘‘She’s painting Roy’s office windows on Wednesday.’’

‘‘An angel scene, if I remember correctly,’’ Gabriel said, studying them carefully.

‘‘What a nice idea.’’ Mercy looked frantically to her friend for help.

‘‘I can’t imagine where she came up with *that* idea.’’ Gabriel’s eyes seemed to bore straight through them.

The three of them huddled close together. ‘‘It’s that time of year, isn’t it?’’ Goodness asked. ‘‘I mean, humans seem to associate Christmas with angels.’’

Mercy spread her wings and stepped forward. "Glory to God in the Highest," she said.

"Glory to God," Shirley echoed.

"Exactly," Goodness said. "We were there to announce the good news to the shepherds that night. Well, not us, exactly, but angels like us."

"I know all about that night, Goodness."

"Of course you do," she said.

"Now, back to the matter of Anne's prayer request."

"Yes, Your Archangelness," Mercy said.

Her friend didn't play the role of innocent well, Goodness thought. She resisted the urge to elbow Mercy since she couldn't do it without being obvious.

"What are your plans?" Gabriel asked, scrutinizing them.

"Funny you should ask," Goodness said. "We were just discussing that. I don't think Roy's going to come right out and ask Julie for a date. He wouldn't be comfortable with such a direct approach."

"He enjoys watching the parade of boats," Gabriel said, flipping through the pages of the book. He looked up again. "Had you considered that?"

It was all Goodness could do not to sidle over and take a peek.

Gabriel's attention returned to the page. "The last couple of Decembers, he's stood on his balcony alone and watched the decorated watercraft float by."

"And he's wished there was someone with him to share the experience," Shirley added. Goodness figured she was just guessing, but she'd probably guessed right.

Gabriel confirmed it. "That wish has been fleeting, but it *is* one he's entertained."

"Julie's so athletic, I'll bet she's a great sailor. She loves the water," Mercy ventured.

"So does Roy," Gabriel said. "Or he did at one time. Unfortunately, he hasn't sailed in years."

"Aimee used to sail with him, didn't she?" Goodness asked, although she was fairly sure she knew the answer.

"Roy sold his sailboat after they split up. He hasn't been out on Puget Sound since."

"How sad for him." Shirley sighed as she said it.

"Perhaps we could—"

"Carry on," Gabriel said. He seemed to be in a hurry now. "You're doing a fine job so far."

"We are?" Goodness couldn't keep herself from saying. "I mean, yes, I know. We're working very hard on this request."

"Good." Then as quickly as he'd come, the Archangel vanished.

Goodness relaxed. Gabriel had yet to recall them from an assignment, but there was always a chance he would, especially with Shirley disobeying the angels' number one rule: no revelations to humans.

Perhaps they were safe, for now at least. She certainly hoped so.

ROY SLEPT BETTER on Monday night than he had in months, possibly years. He always fell asleep easily enough but then he'd wake up two or three hours later. Often he roamed around his condo for much of the night, unable to get back to sleep. During the past few years, he'd tried any number of remedies, all of them useless.

As the alarm sounded, he rolled over and stared at the clock, astonished that he'd slept the entire night uninterrupted. That never happened, at least not anymore.

Roy felt rested and refreshed as he stepped into the shower. He stopped short when he realized he was humming a Christmas carol. Christmas music? Him? Something was going on, and he wasn't sure what. Thrusting his face under the spray, he let the water hit him full force. It occurred to him that his good night's sleep was because of the evening spent with Julie. He liked her. Julie Wilcoff was different from any woman he'd ever known. His money didn't impress her, that was for sure. And she didn't seem to care about his position in the business world. If any other woman had behaved this way, he would have assumed she was pretending, but Julie was genuine. Even a cynic like him could recognize that much.

Roy had often been the target of women looking for a free ride. He saw himself as reasonably wealthy and reasonably attractive; he knew he could date just about anyone he wanted. However, the idea of dating any woman after Aimee had become repugnant to him. Until Julie. He wasn't convinced he liked this, wasn't convinced he was making the right move or that he was interested in making any move at all.

When Roy arrived at the office, it seemed his entire staff was watching him. He felt their eyes on him as he strode through the lobby and toward the elevator. People turned and stared, and he heard a few hushed and badly disguised whispers. He resisted the urge to stop and ask, "What?"

Once inside his office, he followed his normal routine. Ms. Johnson phoned to remind him of a meeting. The Griffin Plastics file remained on his desk and he picked it up reluctantly. He decided he needed more information before making a final decision.

"Could you ask Dean Wilcoff to be available after my meeting?" Roy asked. "I'd like to talk to him."

"I'll see to it right away."

"Thank you."

She hesitated as if she'd never heard him offer his appreciation before. "Will that be all, Mr. Fletcher?"

"Yes." He hung up the phone and leaned back in his soft leather chair, folding his hands. Something was in the air, something he couldn't explain. He didn't know *what* was different, but there was definitely a change, and it wasn't just him.

The meeting, concerning the launch of a new line of security software for home computers, ran smoothly. Roy hurried back to his office when it ended, and Dean Wilcoff arrived a few minutes later. "You asked to see me?" the man said as Ms. Johnson showed him in. He certainly didn't waste any time, Roy observed. He got right to the point.

"I did. Sit down." Roy gestured to the chair across from his desk. He wanted to talk to Wilcoff, but the matter wasn't business-related. Julie had been on his mind from the moment he'd left her last night, and he realized he knew very little about her. They'd talked, but she wasn't one to dwell on herself, unlike a lot of women he'd known. Most wanted to impress him. Julie had surprised him in that way, too.

Dean sat close to the edge of the cushion, apparently ill at ease.

"Did Julie mention we had dinner together last

night?'' Dean had called Julie to say he'd be home late, so Roy had left before Dean's return.

''She did,'' Roy's head of security answered stiffly.

''How old is Julie?'' Roy had never thought to inquire, not that it was important.

Dean stiffened. ''You should ask my daughter that, sir.''

Ever respectful, Roy noted, and unwilling to mingle his personal life with his professional one. He tried another tactic. ''While we were having pizza, Julie told me she's a twin.''

Dean nodded but offered no additional information.

''I gave her a ride home from the office last night,'' Roy said, testing the waters, wading in a little deeper this time.

''So she said.''

''I tried to get her to accept my settlement offer.''

Dean didn't respond.

''She refused.''

''My daughter's over twenty-one and makes her own decisions,'' Dean informed him.

''As she should.'' Roy certainly agreed with that.

Dean met his eyes. ''I've asked her to apologize for her behavior yesterday.''

This should be interesting. ''And she agreed?'' Frankly, Roy would be surprised if she did. He'd tried to talk sense into her over pizza and she'd been as stubborn as ever. Judging by her dogged refusal,

Roy didn't expect her to change her mind about his offer anytime soon.

"Julie said she'd give the matter of an apology some thought."

Roy smiled. So she hadn't ruled it out altogether. He admired her for that.

"Is there anything else?" Wilcoff asked, transparently eager to leave.

"Yes. Did I tell you my mother will be here at some point on Wednesday?"

"You did." Dean stood. "You said she'd be painting the lobby windows."

Roy stood, too. "I'll check in with you later about Julie."

"What about her?"

Roy realized he'd spoken out of turn. "About… whether she decides to apologize or not."

"That's up to my daughter."

"Yes, of course. No reflection on your job performance, Dean, which to this point has been excellent."

"Thank you."

Roy nodded, dismissing the other man.

Dean moved to the door, then turned and met Roy's gaze. "Are you romantically interested in my daughter?"

Roy's throat went dry. Romantically interested in Julie? Instinct told him to deny it immediately, but he wasn't sure. "Would it bother you if I was?"

"Again, that's my daughter's business. And yours."

"Yes, it is," Roy agreed. Theirs and nobody else's.

SHIRLEY AND GOODNESS, hovering above the office, nudged each other. Mercy gave them a thumbs-up and a big grin.

Kudos to Dean, they all decided, for having the nerve to ask.

Romantically interested? Yes!

CHAPTER ELEVEN

ANNE WAS ENJOYING herself. Paintbrush in hand, she stood in the large lobby of her son's office building and spread the bright colors across the smooth glass, creating a festive greeting for all to see. She'd drawn the outlines with a felt-tip pen and was now filling in the figures, using acrylic paints.

This was the first Christmas season since the divorce that she'd actually felt like celebrating. It wasn't an effort; nothing felt forced, least of all her happiness. She thanked the angel for that. The one who'd appeared to her. Everything had changed for the better that day. Her heart felt lighter, less burdened, and life suddenly seemed good and right again.

After all these years, her prayer request had apparently been heard. Even now, Anne couldn't get over the glorious, wonderful sound of her son's laughter. Such a minor joy had felt forever lost to both of them. Even more wonderful, a woman—the first one her son had mentioned in five years—had caused this spark of excitement in her son.

"How does that look, Jason?" Anne asked the security guard. The young man certainly took his duties seriously. The entire time she'd been painting, Jason had watched her. He must have been told that no one was to bother her, and he made sure she was left alone with her painting.

Jason didn't answer and Anne turned around to see him studying the parking lot.

"Trouble?" Anne asked.

"Perhaps it'd be best if you left the area, ma'am."

Anne peered outside; the only person she could see was a young woman wearing what appeared to be a soccer uniform. She was walking toward the building. "Who's that?" Anne asked.

"Julie Wilcoff," Jason answered in a low voice. He moved from behind the desk and stood directly in front of the glass doors, his posture a warning in itself.

Anne watched as the woman paused outside the door and smiled at the security guard. "Jason, I'm here to talk to my father."

"I'm not falling for that a second time," he said. "Your father told me to keep you out of this building and he hasn't told me anything different, so I'm keeping you out."

The woman glanced impatiently toward Anne and then back to the security guard. "Jason, please."

"If you've got a problem with that," the guard said matter-of-factly, "then I suggest you take it up with your father."

Ms. Wilcoff promptly pulled a cell phone out of

her pocket, punched a few numbers and held it to her ear.

Jason stood exactly where he was.

"Is this the girl who gave my son such a talking-to the other day?" Anne asked. If so, Anne was eager to meet her.

"Yes, ma'am."

"Her father banned her from the building?"

"I believe Mr. Fletcher gave his approval, ma'am."

Anne's spirits did an abrupt dive. "I'm sure he's had a change of heart," she said, praying she was right.

"Then he'll need to tell me that himself, ma'am." The guard wasn't budging, not an inch. No way, no how. That much was obvious.

Julie Wilcoff seemed to have trouble reaching her father. With an air of frustration, she clicked off the cell phone. "My father isn't answering," she called from the other side of the door.

"That isn't my problem."

"He *asked* to see me," she insisted.

For a moment it seemed Jason might waver, but he held his ground. "He didn't say anything to me about that. I don't have any option but to do as I've been instructed. You aren't allowed in this building. I'm sorry, Ms. Wilcoff, but I have my orders."

Julie nodded. "I understand. Will you tell my father I was by?"

"If I see him," Jason promised.

Julie nodded again and turned around. She started back toward the parking lot, walking at a quick pace.

Anne refused to let this woman leave.

Jason moved from his post and Anne rushed to the door. ''Ms. Wilcoff? Julie?''

Julie glanced over her shoulder.

Anne stood in the doorway and gave her a quick wave. ''I'm Anne Fletcher, Roy's mother.''

''Oh, hi,'' she said. Turning again, she stopped in her progress toward the visitors' parking lot. ''It's a pleasure to meet you. I guess you heard about your son's and my disagreement.'' The wind whipped the hair about her face, and Julie swept it away with one stroke of her hand. ''I actually came to see Roy, but I needed to talk to my dad first. I can see that's impossible.''

''No, it isn't.'' Anne raised her index finger. ''Wait just a minute.'' She closed the door and discovered Jason frowning at her. ''I can't let her in here, Mrs. Fletcher,'' he said, ''so don't go asking me to make allowances.''

''I had no intention of doing that.'' She planned to take another approach altogether. ''The best thing to do is contact my son and get this settled once and for all.''

Jason said nothing.

''Can I use the phone on your desk?'' She didn't have a cell phone; it was an expense she couldn't afford.

''Go ahead.'' He kept his gaze pinned to the door

as if he half feared Julie might try to dash in while he wasn't looking.

Anne walked over to the desk and called Ms. Johnson, her son's assistant. ''Hello, Eleanor,'' she said as if they were old friends. ''Could I speak to my son?''

The woman hesitated. ''I'm sorry, Mrs. Fletcher, but he's in a meeting.''

''A meeting,'' Anne repeated. She'd long suspected that was the excuse Roy used when he wasn't in the mood to deal with her. ''Did he ask you to say that?'' she whispered.

''Not this time,'' his assistant admitted, confirming Anne's suspicions. ''He actually is in a meeting.''

''Oh, dear,'' Anne said, breathing a sigh.

''Is there anything I can do?''

Anne chewed her lower lip. ''Do you happen to know Julie Wilcoff?''

''I do.'' Eleanor's voice grew warm and excited. ''She's here.''

''In the building?''

''No, the security guard won't let her inside. Apparently there's some edict her father gave and she's forbidden to come into the building. Is that true?''

''I'm afraid it must be, but we all like Ms. Wilcoff.''

Unfortunately, Jason hadn't gotten that memo, Anne mused. ''Any idea on how we can get her inside to see my son?''

After another second's hesitation, Roy's assistant said, "I'll be down directly."

"Oh, thank you," Anne murmured. She looked up and saw Jason frowning at her. Julie hadn't moved from her position outside the doors.

"What did he say?"

"I didn't speak to my son, but Ms. Johnson is on her way down."

Jason frowned even more fiercely and shook his head. "That isn't good enough. It's got to be Mr. Wilcoff or Mr. Fletcher himself. No one else. As I explained earlier, I have my orders."

Anne ignored him and went back to the glass entrance doors. She opened one and said, "I phoned Roy, but he's in a meeting. His assistant is coming down to see what she can do."

"It's all right, Mrs. Fletcher. I'll just come back another time."

Anne's arm shot out the door. "No! Stay where you are. I'll be right back." She turned away and then immediately turned around. "Promise me you won't leave!" If she was going to make a fool of herself, she wanted to be sure it was worth her while.

Julie grinned. "I won't leave."

"Thank you."

Anne addressed Jason next. "When Ms. Johnson arrives, tell her that I've gone to get my son." She refused to let this opportunity—or this woman—disappear from Roy's life. With a determination that surprised even her, Anne marched over to the elevator and pushed the button. When the car didn't come fast enough to suit her, she pushed it again.

A high-tech buzzing finally announced the elevator. To her relief, it was empty, and she shot to the top floor in what felt like seconds. Stepping off, she hurried into the foyer, glancing around. Ms. Johnson, as Anne knew, wasn't at her desk. Anne thought she heard voices at the end of the hallway and headed in that direction.

Sure enough, there was a meeting taking place in the conference room. Anne remembered seeing it when Roy gave her a tour shortly after moving into the building.

She hated to barge in, but there was nothing else to be done. Knocking politely at the door, Anne walked inside, her smock smeared with paint and her hair a mess. The room, which had been lively with conversation, went silent. Twenty or so men and women, all important-looking, sat around a long, rectangular table. Every one of them turned to stare at her. Anne smiled weakly and noticed that Roy was standing at the front of the room.

''Mother?''

''Could I speak to you a moment?''

He raised his eyebrows. ''Now?''

Anne held her breath. ''Please.''

Roy gestured apologetically at his associates. ''If you'll excuse me?''

They all nodded and Roy walked to the back of the room. "What is it, Mother?"

From the way his eyes flared and the even, unemotional tone of his voice, Anne could tell he wasn't pleased. He guided her, none too gently, into the hallway.

"I'm so sorry to interrupt you," she said, clasping her hands tightly.

"If this has to do with the Christmas scene on the windows, then—"

"Oh, no," she insisted, "it's not about that." Her throat felt dry and it was difficult to concentrate. "This has to do with Jason..."

"And exactly who is Jason?"

"The security guard downstairs. He tells me Julie Wilcoff has been banned from the building. I know it was her father's doing, but Jason seems to believe you supported that decision. Did you?"

His demeanor changed, and his mouth and eyes softened. "I might have. Why?"

"She's here."

"Now?"

Anne nodded. "Jason won't let her in to speak to you."

"She came to see me, did she?" He folded his arms and seemed to consider this information with some amusement. Then the humor left his eyes. "Did she give you any indication *why* she wanted to speak to me?"

Anne shook her head. "Not really."

His mouth twitched. Was that a smile trying to emerge? "Ms. Johnson did her best to talk Jason into letting her in, but he won't budge."

"I'll call him myself," Roy promised. "Go ahead and have Ms. Johnson bring Julie up to my office. Tell her I'll be there in fifteen minutes." He frowned at his watch. "Make that twenty."

"I hope I did the right thing," Anne said.

"You did exactly the right thing," he said, and to her utter amazement, he took her by the shoulders and kissed her cheek.

Anne hurried downstairs. Jason was on the phone when she got off the elevator. He muttered something that sounded like "yessir," replaced the receiver and walked over to the glass door, holding it open for Julie.

"You can come in now," he told the young woman, who remained standing outside.

Julie walked into the building slowly, as if she expected alarms to ring the instant she stepped over the threshold.

"Thank you," she said to Anne.

"Mr. Fletcher would like you to wait in his office," Ms. Johnson told her.

"I'll be up in a moment," Julie said. She turned to Anne and the Christmas scene she'd started painting on the windows. "You painted these angels?"

"Oh…yes." Anne had almost forgotten the reason she was in the lobby at all. She'd painted three angels this time, floating on a cloud and looking down over Bethlehem and the manger scene. The angels dominated the painting, their joy at the Savior's birth evident.

"They're absolutely lovely," Julie said.

"Thank you."

"I had plenty of time to look at them while I was waiting, and they seem almost real to me."

Anne blushed with pleasure. "How kind you are."

"Roy mentioned you were an artist. You're obviously very talented."

"Roy mentioned me?"

"Yes, although I don't know him well." Julie shrugged. "We definitely got off on the wrong foot. I'm here to talk to him and, well, I hope we can start again."

Anne gripped Julie's hand in both of hers. "I hope you can, too. Could—could you and I talk sometime?"

Julie smiled. "I'd like that very much."

"So would I," Anne said. "I'll be in touch."

CHAPTER TWELVE

JULIE WAS WAITING in his office when Roy returned from the meeting, which he'd adjourned rather quickly. She sat in the chair across from his desk, looking unusually demure. His mood had improved from the moment he learned she'd come here to see him. He'd been thinking of her ever since their pizza dinner, and he'd wondered if he'd see her again soon. He had his answer and frankly, it was one he liked.

"Julie." He greeted her warmly, walking over to his desk and sitting behind it. "This is a pleasant surprise."

"I hope I'm not disturbing you." She'd apparently come to his office immediately after school, not bothering to change into street clothes first. Despite the weather, she wore shorts and a sports jersey, and a whistle dangled like a long necklace around her neck.

"Not really. What can I do for you?"

He assumed she was there to accept his settlement; she didn't need to show up in person, but he was delighted she had. So she was like everyone else—willing to take easy money. Yes, he was a little disillusioned, but he still liked her. He couldn't blame Julie Wilcoff for a quality shared by practically every other person on Earth. Greed was part of human nature, and he'd long since reconciled himself to that.

"I came to talk about what happened on Monday," she said simply. "My father felt I was out of line bursting in here the way I did."

"You were angry."

"Angry," she repeated, and with a soft chuckle added, "You have no idea. I don't think I've ever been more insulted than—" She bit off the rest of her thought. "At any rate, Dad's right. I should never have reacted like that. I made a fool of myself."

Roy was quite enjoying this. "So you've had a change of heart. Somehow, I knew you would."

"A change of heart?"

He didn't know why she insisted on denying the obvious. Certainly, the settlement was foremost in her mind; it had to be. "I'm talking about the money."

Julie frowned and shook her head. "This has nothing to do with money. It has to do with an apology."

"You're *not* here because of the settlement?" He wasn't fooled, but decided to play along for the time being.

"I came to apologize for storming into your office and for the things I said. I am not here about that stupid, insulting settlement offer, which I have repeatedly rejected. I'd think that by now you'd get the message.'' With a visible effort, she managed to keep her anger in check.

Roy's own anger was rising. ''Everyone's interested in money, Julie, so don't even bother pretending otherwise. Let's both be honest, shall we? You aren't going to get a better offer, so just sign the papers my attorney mailed you and be done with it.''

''I believe I already told you what I think of that settlement,'' she muttered. She slid closer to the edge of the upholstered chair. Soon she was barely perched on the cushion at all. He thought she might be in danger of slipping onto the floor.

''You're holding out for more money, aren't you?''

She bolted to her feet as if someone had pinched her. ''You're impossible, you know that? I came here in good faith—''

''Good faith?'' Roy didn't see it that way. Not when she said one thing and wanted another. But ultimately, human nature at its most basic couldn't be defeated.

''I thought we'd made some progress, you and I, and…well, I can see you're hopeless.''

''Me?'' he shouted. ''*You're* the one who's got her eye on the almighty dollar.''

''I don't want any of your stupid money! Why can't you get that through your head?''

"Because you're no different from any other woman."

Her eyes seemed to grow wider. "Now you're insulting not only me but every woman alive."

"Yes, well, if the shoes fits."

Hands on her hips, Julie glared at him. "Then I guess you know what you can do with your shoe."

He glared right back. Standing, he reached for his phone and punched in the number for security. "Please send somebody to escort Ms. Wilcoff from the building."

Julie's mouth sagged open in what appeared to be shock. "Thank you very much, but I can see myself out." She started for the open door, arms swinging at her sides, every step filled with righteous indignation. She got halfway across the room before she swung around and said, "I really tried, you know."

"Julie, just sign the settlement." They would put an end to this, once and for all. Then they could move on, maybe explore the possibilities between them. He'd be willing to overlook this flaw; no doubt he had flaws of his own. Naiveté about the motives of others didn't happen to be one of them. "Just sign, okay?" he said wearily.

"No!"

Well, that answered that.

"Furthermore, I think you're—"

"Uh-uh," Roy said, holding up his finger. "You don't want to say something you'll regret later."

The elevator doors opened before Julie had a

chance to insult him. Jason, the guard from downstairs, loomed in the doorway. "You asked for security, Mr. Fletcher?"

If looks could kill, Roy would be six feet under. As best he could, he ignored Julie's death-dealing glare. "I did."

Jason gripped Julie by the elbow. "Once she's gone, is she allowed back in the building?"

Julie closed her eyes. Roy looked at her curiously—was she grinding her teeth? For whatever reason, the anger seemed to drain from her.

"Let's play that part by ear," Roy told the guard. When she saw that she had no choice but to sign, then and only then would Roy be willing to see her. He insisted on at least that much honesty.

Julie resumed glaring at him. "I've destroyed the papers your attorney mailed, and I will destroy any replacement papers."

"This is my final offer."

She grinned. "I should hope so." Still in Jason's firm grip, she turned and walked away. "Goodbye," she said over her shoulder. "And I mean that."

"I'll see to it she leaves the building," Jason assured Roy as he hustled her out the door.

"Thank you." Roy reclaimed his chair. Their conversation hadn't gone the way he'd wanted. He'd hoped they could find some common ground. His problem, he realized, was that he genuinely liked Julie. Okay, so she was a little stubborn and clearly unreasonable. But now he was afraid he might never see her again, judging by that final goodbye. She'd probably just mail the signed attorney's contract, disgruntled that her ploy to get more hadn't succeeded. She'd settle for twenty-five thousand and she'd avoid him from this moment on.

The thought depressed him. Besides, he was in the right. It was Julie who'd been unreasonable, not him.

He returned his attention to a number of pressing business matters, determined to put Julie out of his mind. Fifteen minutes later, he began to pace, unable to concentrate. Fifteen minutes after that, he called Ms. Johnson into his office.

"Sit down," he instructed his assistant when she entered the room.

Eyeing him as he walked from one end of his office to the other, Ms. Johnson slowly lowered herself into the chair opposite his desk. "Is everything all right, Mr. Fletcher?"

"What makes you ask?" he muttered irritably.

She looked embarrassed now and her gaze followed him across the room. "I don't think I've ever seen you so...agitated."

"I'm not agitated," he barked.

She dropped her gaze. "As you say."

Roy resisted the urge to argue with her to prove his point. He sank down in his chair, tempted to explain that he was the same as he'd always been. But why bother? Women always stuck together.

"You wanted to see me?" Ms. Johnson murmured.

Roy nodded and steepled his fingers as he leaned forward and rested his elbows on his desk. "I have a question and I'd appreciate your honesty."

"Yes, sir."

Again Roy felt her hesitation. He wasn't convinced she was the best person to ask, but his options were limited. "Am I an unreasonable man?" He didn't know exactly why he was questioning his own behavior, his own perceptions. Was there the slightest chance he was wrong in his beliefs about Julie?

Ms. Johnson's shoulders rose and then fell in a soundless sigh. "You can be at times," she said, obviously uncomfortable meeting his gaze.

"I see," he said. "Can you give me an example?"

She nodded. "Just now with Julie Wilcoff."

Roy was afraid she was going to say that. "You think *I'm* the unreasonable one?" *Women stick together,* he reminded himself.

"Mr. Fletcher, perhaps it would be better if you discussed this with someone else, someone more… appropriate."

Roy frowned, unable to imagine who else he could approach. "I asked you."

His assistant edged forward. "I had a chance to talk to Ms. Wilcoff while you were finishing up the Griffin meeting, and she seemed sincere to me. I know it was difficult for her to come, but out of respect for her father, she felt it was the right thing to do."

"She had a rotten attitude," he snapped.

"If you don't mind my saying so, it appears you're the one with the attitude problem."

His irritation flared briefly and then died.

"Not once did she mention the settlement," Ms. Johnson continued. "If I were to guess, I'd say she completely forgot about it. I believe she came here for precisely the reason she said—to apologize for bursting into the office. She admitted there were better ways of handling the situation and she felt badly about it. I think she was afraid she'd embarrassed her father."

"The only person she embarrassed was herself," Roy said.

"At least she was woman enough to admit it."

Roy looked thoughtfully at his executive assistant. She'd spoken frankly in ways he'd never expected. "What are you suggesting?"

"I'm saying that perhaps it's time..." She hesitated.

"Go on," he urged. He might as well hear it all.

"Perhaps," his assistant said, "you should talk to Julie about this."

Roy nodded, swallowing hard. Perhaps she was right.

WHEN SHE WAS this angry, this perturbed, the best thing for Julie to do was run—as if a pack of wolves was after her. The minute she was home, she tossed aside her shorts and changed into her running gear. After a few perfunctory warm-up exercises, she took off. As her shoes hit the pavement, her thoughts chased each other around and around. Six miles passed, six pounding, breathless miles, before she found some measure of serenity. By then, her calves ached and her lungs burned. It was pitch-dark as she ran back to her neighborhood, cheered by the bright display of Christmas lights on the homes along her route.

As she rounded the corner to her house, she noticed a dark sedan parked in front. Her father was home, too; she saw his light-blue car parked in the garage beside hers, the door left open.

Instead of waiting for her inside the house, Roy Fletcher sat on the top porch step. She came up the walkway, bent over and braced her hands against her knees as she caught her breath. "What are you doing here?" she asked between gasps. If he wanted to continue their argument, she would simply walk into the house and slam the door.

Roy stood and brushed his hands against his sides. "I don't know. It seemed like a nice afternoon for a drive."

"Sure it did," she said sarcastically, still breathing hard.

"Would you believe I just happened to be in the neighborhood?"

She shook her head.

''All right,'' he said. ''Ms. Johnson suggested the two of us talk.''

''Talk...'' Julie straightened. She wouldn't have believed it if she hadn't seen it herself. The great Mr. Roy Fletcher was here to make peace.

''This time I was the one out of line.'' Apologies didn't come naturally to this man; it sounded as if the words stuck in his throat.

Julie gazed into his eyes to see if she could judge his sincerity. As far as she could tell, he meant it. She smiled and offered him her hand. He took it, then smiled back—a smile that was warm and lazy and completely sexy.

''Furthermore, I'm willing to make up for my rudeness,'' he told her.

''Really? And how do you intend to do that?''

''Dinner?''

''When?''

He pulled a PalmPilot out of his pocket and looked up to meet her eyes. ''What about tonight?''

Although tempted, Julie already had dinner in the Crock-Pot and test papers to grade. ''Another night would be better.''

He frowned, then suggested, ''Friday? That works for me.''

''Sorry, I've got a game.''

''What sort of game?''

''I'm the girls' soccer coach.''

"Oh." He scrolled down his appointment calendar. "Saturday evening is free from seven o'clock on."

"Yes, but..." Julie paused, biting her lip. "Isn't that the parade of ships?" This was one of her favorite Christmas traditions. Last year, together with her father, Julie had managed to get her mother down to the waterfront. It had been a highlight of the season for so many years, and she hated to miss it. Especially now, when the event held such a significant memory for her.

Roy glanced up. "Yes, I believe Saturday night is the annual Christmas parade of ships."

"I don't suppose you'd care to see that, would you?" she asked hesitantly.

"Actually I would. I have a good view of Lake Washington from my condo if you'd like to see it from there."

"Dinner, too?"

Grinning, he nodded.

"Wonderful." Julie was thrilled not only with the opportunity to view the boats festooned with their Christmas lights but to know Roy better. His coming here was encouraging. Then a thought sobered her. They continued to trip over the matter of that damn settlement again and again. "You have to agree to one thing first."

"All right, let's hear it."

She squared her shoulders. "If you say a word about the settlement or mention money even once, I'm out of there."

He seemed about to argue. ''If you insist,'' he finally said.

''I do.''

''Then I guess I have to agree.''

''Good.'' She smiled and raised both hands, palms up. ''See? That wasn't so hard now, was it?''

''As a matter of fact,'' he said with another grin, ''it was.''

Julie laughed, walking past him and into the house. She opened the front door and glanced over her shoulder, silently inviting him inside. ''I should probably ask my father to escort you from the house, just so you know how it feels.''

''Yes, well—''

''Never mind.'' Her father sat in the living room reading the evening newspaper. He lowered it as Julie walked in, Roy Fletcher a few steps behind.

''Dad, make Mr. Fletcher welcome while I shower, okay?''

Her father's eyes widened. ''What's this?''

''We made peace,'' Julie explained.

Dean looked at Julie and then his employer. ''Somehow, I knew you would.'' He set his newspaper aside. ''Do you play poker, Mr. Fletcher?''

''Now and then. I might be a little rusty.''

''Oh, that's not a problem.'' Her father rubbed his hands together and gave a stagy wink. ''I'll get a deck.''

CHAPTER THIRTEEN

ANNE COULDN'T STOP smiling. Everything was working out so well between her son and Julie Wilcoff. With Eleanor Johnson, Roy's assistant, feeding her information, Anne had learned that he'd gone to Julie's yesterday afternoon—even though he'd thrown her out of his office. Her son had actually sought out this delightful and strong-willed young woman.

That alone was enough to make Anne weak with joy, but then she'd found out that Roy had gone a step further and asked Julie for a date. He'd invited her to his home on Saturday! Ms. Johnson was busy contacting caterers. He was having Julie over for dinner, and then they were going to watch the Christmas parade of ships.

This was almost more than Anne had dared to hope, the best early Christmas gift she could ever receive.

Although Anne had only met Julie briefly, she'd taken an instant liking to the young woman. She wasn't at all what Anne had expected, although that didn't matter. Julie was nearly as tall as her son and solidly built, but as Anne had learned a long time ago, it was character and not appearance that counted. Roy had fallen for a pretty face and an empty heart once, and he'd suffered the consequences. So had Anne....

"Oh, my," she murmured aloud, irritated with herself. Describing Julie as "solid" made her sound dumpy and unattractive, and nothing could be further from the truth. She just wasn't Aimee, who was petite and blond and delicate. Julie was none of those things, and all for the better. Besides, *solid* applied to her character, solid and direct, unlike Aimee's wispy charm.

Anne had spent a second day at the office, finishing her angels. Home now, her spirits soaring, she stood barefoot in the kitchen chopping vegetables for a huge salad when the phone rang. She automatically checked her caller ID and noticed the New York area code.

It could only be Marta.

"Hello," Anne said, pleased to hear from her friend. The possibility that the angel painting might sell for an astronomical eight thousand dollars—or more—had set her heart racing with hope and excitement.

"Anne, it's Marta. How are you?"

"Fabulous! I can't tell you how good it was to see you. I've been feeling great ever since."

"I'm glad," Marta said.

"How are you?" Anne was concerned about her friend's marital situation.

"I'm doing fine."

Somehow Anne doubted that. "And Jack?"

Marta hesitated. "He's still being Jack."

Anne knew then. Marta hadn't confronted her husband, because the potential aftermath of bringing the truth into the open outweighed the pain. Anne certainly didn't blame Marta. Not so long ago she'd faced a similar situation; she understood and sympathized.

"I'm calling about the painting," Marta said brightly. A little too brightly.

Anne held her breath. "Did my angel sell?"

"It's not for sale," Marta said flatly.

Taken aback, Anne said nothing.

"Paintings are always more attractive when the artist refuses to sell them, my dear."

"Oh." To Anne's way of thinking, that was dishonest.

"It *is* your personal favorite, isn't that correct?"

"Yes, but..." Eight thousand dollars was almost a year's worth of mortgage payments. Anne had begun to hope, to do something she'd told herself she never would, and that was to count on selling one of her paintings. "I *would* like to sell the angel...."

"But only if the price is right."

"Well, yes..."

"That's what I told her."

"Her?"

"Mrs. Gould. She's one of the Berkshire Goulds. She's got oodles and oodles of money."

"She likes my angel?" Anne was almost afraid to hope.

"Likes her?" Marta asked, laughing. "Evelyn is determined to have her, but I refused to sell. I explained the situation and told her I needed to discuss the matter with you first."

"Has she offered eight thousand dollars?"

"No."

Anne's heart fell. If an extremely wealthy woman hadn't offered that much for a painting she supposedly wanted, then perhaps she wasn't interested, after all.

"She offered more." Marta giggled.

"Ten thousand?" Anne whispered.

"More."

"And you turned her *down?*"

"Of course I did. I had to confer with you. Besides, if we caved too easily, she might suspect you really wanted to sell it in the first place."

"Oh, Marta, I don't know if we're doing the right thing."

"Trust me, Anne. I've been in this business for years. I know how to work this buyer. Furthermore, my commission from this sale is my Christmas gift to you."

Anne was astonished. "I can't let you do that!"

"Yes, you can and you will."

"But I want to make it on my own, Marta." This was one of the very reasons Anne had chosen to paint under the name of Mary Flemming. She didn't want her friends' charity.

"If you knew Mrs. Gould, you'd know that she's—"

"I'm talking about the commission."

The line went silent for a moment. "Actually," Marta confessed, "I might end up moving in with you at some point, and I was hoping to pave the way in case that happened."

"You're serious?" Sometimes with Marta it was hard to tell.

"Very."

"But you haven't confronted Jack?"

Anne heard Marta's sigh. "I've tried, and every time I broach the subject, it's as if Jack knows what's coming and starts talking about something else. Once he simply got up and left the room. I'm so damned emotional about it. All I seem to do is cry and then I get so angry with Jack and with myself that I'm a worthless mess."

"Of course you're emotional!" Anne cried. "You have every right to be."

"I trusted Jack."

Anne had trusted Burton, too. Although she was reluctant to mention it, Anne felt she'd be doing her friend a disservice if she didn't share the painful lesson she'd learned. "Keep an eye on your finances." She hated to give her more to worry about, but this was the trap Anne had fallen into, at great cost to herself.

"Jack would never—"

"I said the same thing about Burton," Anne told her. "What you need to remember is that if Jack's untrustworthy in one area, he could be untrustworthy in others, too."

"Like Burton?"

Anne swallowed around the lump blocking her throat. "Like Burton," she repeated.

"How much did he cheat you out of?"

Anne didn't want to think about it, didn't want to confess how blind and foolish she'd been. "A quarter of a million dollars is my best estimate."

"Oh, my," Marta breathed. "That much?"

"I'm past the anger now."

"But how can you be?" she demanded, outraged on Anne's behalf.

"What else can I do? Hate him? Do you honestly think Burton cares how I feel about him?" Anne had gone through all of this after the divorce, gone through it over and over again. "It wouldn't matter. The only person I'd be hurting is myself."

"But you must've had some feelings?"

"Of course I did. In the beginning I was angry, and then I was so hurt I couldn't stop crying. For a while, I wondered if it was even worth living."

"Oh, Anne."

She'd never told anyone about those dark, ugly thoughts. Anne wondered if she was doing the right thing now in confessing how bleak everything had seemed during those first dreadful months. When she'd discovered how bad her financial situation was, she'd sunk to her lowest depths. Once she'd learned she could cope with even that, her sense of self had begun to reassert itself.

"Frankly, I would've wanted to kill him."

Anne laughed. "I considered that, but I didn't want to spend the rest of my life in a jail cell."

Marta laughed, too, but there was little humor in it.

"You want advice?" Anne was reluctant to give it, but she'd been in the same position Marta was now. She knew that her friend probably hadn't been ready to hear her suggestions when they'd spoken the week before. She also knew how difficult it was to make decisions and think clearly during any kind of crisis.

"Please." Marta's voice was as soft as a whisper.

"If I were going through it again, the first thing I'd do is see an attorney and have our joint assets frozen."

Marta's breath came in a rush. "You told me to see one when I met you in Seattle, but now? So soon?"

"The sooner the better."

"Okay," Marta said, her voice gaining conviction. "I can do that."

"A good one, preferably not one you both know."

"All right." Marta hesitated. "Should I tell Jack what I've done?"

To be fair to both parties, Anne felt she should. "I would. In your own time. It doesn't have to be confrontational."

"Something simple, in other words, like...like, I know what you're doing and I've seen an attorney. Period. End of story."

"Something like that."

"All right, I'll do it." Marta sounded determined now.

Anne longed to put her arms around her friend and offer her reassurance and comfort. Marta, so experienced and sophisticated, was as emotionally vulnerable as Anne had been.

"Call me the minute you know anything," Anne said, trying to encourage her.

"About the painting?"

Anne had forgotten about her angel. "That, too, but right now I'm more concerned that you take care of yourself."

"I...I think I'll wait until after the holidays," Marta said. "To see an attorney, I mean."

"Don't," Anne warned. "Do it today, before you lose your nerve."

"You're right, you're right. I will."

"And stay in touch," Anne said.

"I will," Marta promised.

Anne hoped she would. But there was nothing more she could say or do. It was Marta's decision.

CHAPTER FOURTEEN

THINGS WERE WORKING OUT nicely, Goodness thought. Despite their differences, Julie and Roy had knocked down some of the roadblocks that stood between them. Although she hadn't admitted it yet, Julie was attracted to Roy. They were having their first official date on Saturday, and the relationship was starting to take shape. Mercy was right, after all. Goodness gave her friend credit. Julie might very well be the answer to Anne's prayer request for her son.

This was the second evening the three angels had hovered over the Wilcoffs' living room while Dean and Roy played two-handed poker. Granted, Dean and not Julie had invited him tonight, since they'd both enjoyed the previous poker game. But Julie hadn't objected. And she'd even made dinner again—black-bean soup, corn bread and a salad. Chatting as he dealt, Dean picked up his two cards for Texas Hold'em and set the deck on the coffee table between them.

Roy looked over his cards and quickly placed his bet. Mercy, a serious student of cards, peered down at his hand.

"Should I help him with the deal?" she whispered.

"No," Goodness cried. It was exactly this sort of intervention that continued to get them in trouble. "Roy can win or lose this game on his own. Besides, I think it would do him good if Dean beat him again."

"Oh, come on," Mercy pleaded. "Don't be such a spoilsport."

Shirley sat atop the light fixture and sighed expressively. "Have you ever noticed how the game of poker is a lot like Roy's life just now?"

Goodness and Mercy stared at her. Sometimes Shirley came up with the most bizarre pronouncements.

"In what way?" Goodness was already certain she was going to regret asking.

"Notice how willing Roy is to fold," Shirley said, pointing to the six and the three, one a spade and the other a heart.

"Well, yes, but if I was dealt those cards in Texas Hold'em, I'd fold, too," Mercy told her. "He doesn't have much opportunity to make anything of it, and Dean has something better."

"Roy's done the same in life," Shirley said. "He's cast his father and Aimee aside. His inability to forgive them, as Anne has done, is a blight on his soul." She shook her head. "Forgiveness is hard, and most people tend to hold on to their hurts, to take some kind of perverse satisfaction in them. I don't understand, but it's the way of humans."

"Roy needs more time," Goodness murmured. Angry and bitter as he was, any kind of positive relationship with his father was impossible. Every effort Burton had made toward reconciliation with his son, Roy had rejected. He wasn't anywhere close to finding forgiveness for either his father or Aimee.

"Perhaps," Shirley agreed, but reluctantly.

"He'll get a better hand next time," Mercy said, peering over Goodness's shoulder, watching as Roy shuffled the deck.

"He needs what humans call luck, and we both know there's no such thing as luck, only God," Goodness reminded them both, but no one seemed to be listening. Both her fellow Prayer Ambassadors were intent on the game.

"Roy needs all the help he can get," Shirley said. "That's why we're here."

"Did you lend him a little heavenly assistance just now?" Goodness demanded when Roy came up with a pair of kings.

First Mercy and now Shirley. The two of them were out of control. Goodness seemed to be the only one with a sense of mission, a sense of purpose. They had important work to accomplish, and her fellow Ambassadors weren't taking it seriously. They seemed more intent on this card game. Not that Goodness was averse to poker, of course, but unlike her colleagues, she did have her priorities straight. Pouting, she folded her wings, crossed her arms and tapped her foot.

Mercy looked up, surprised at this uncharacteristic display of temper. "I didn't have anything to do with him getting that pair."

"Me, neither," Shirley said with an expression of such innocence that Goodness had no choice but to believe her. "I'm just saying Roy could do with a good turn of the cards, but I wasn't responsible for that one."

"Oh, all right," Goodness muttered. She was tired of policing her friends. And at least they seemed to be realigning their priorities.

The phone rang. "Who's that?" Mercy asked.

"Quiet," Goodness said. "Julie's answering it."

Both Shirley and Mercy flew around while Goodness hovered in the kitchen doorway, listening in on the conversation. "It's Anne," she said excitedly.

"How'd she get Julie's phone number?" Shirley asked.

"I don't know."

"Probably the phone book," Mercy suggested.

"What does she want?"

"Shh," Goodness cautioned. This was wonderful! She beamed at her friends. "Anne's inviting her to lunch."

"When?"

"Saturday."

"She's having dinner with Roy on Saturday," Mercy said with a worried frown.

Goodness motioned for them to be quiet, fast losing her patience. This was hard enough without the two of them pestering her. Mercy planted both hands over her mouth, while Shirley whirled about the room like a hamster on a treadmill.

"Well?" Shirley said when Goodness left the kitchen doorway.

"They're meeting on the Seattle waterfront."

"I *love* the waterfront," Mercy said.

Goodness looked at her. "Promise me you won't start throwing those salmon again."

"I'm not making any such promise."

"Need I remind you that we're on a mission?"

Shirley nodded sternly. "A very important mission."

Goodness noticed how Mercy glanced longingly at the deck of cards and the piles of chips. She found it far too easy to get distracted. Maybe her priorities weren't quite in order yet.

JULIE GATHERED the team of junior-high girls around her. Huddling close together to ward off the December-afternoon cold, her soccer team radiated energy and enthusiasm. Each girl thrust her right arm into the center of the huddle and gave a loud cheer.

The first string raced onto the field for the opening kick, and the others returned to the bench. As Julie started down the sideline, she glanced into the stadium. A number of parents had already arrived.

More would come later in the game, depending on work schedules. The girls appreciated the support and so did Julie.

She had several talented players. Most of the girls had been involved with soccer from the age of five, and they knew how to play as a team. At halftime, they were ahead three to two.

Their audience had grown, Julie saw as she sent her girls back onto the field for the second half of the game. Darkness descended earlier and earlier these days, and the field lights came on automatically. As they did, she noticed a lone figure standing by the chain-link fence at the far end of the field. *It couldn't be.* Roy Fletcher? Surely she was mistaken. Why would he attend one of her games?

Julie felt the blood rush to her face and then quickly drain away. He'd been to the house for dinner two nights in a row, and played cards with her father both times. He'd apparently enjoyed the meals, although she'd never thought of Roy Fletcher as the kind of man who'd appreciate a bowl of black-bean soup and buttery corn bread. He'd surprised her by accepting and then eating two big bowlfuls, all the while praising her cooking skills. He'd been equally enthusiastic about Wednesday's Crock-Pot stew. Now he'd shown up at her soccer game.

The two teams were tied in the third quarter, but Abraham Lincoln managed to pull off a win with a last-second goal, ending the match with a score of four to three. Julie went into the locker room with the team, but she didn't expect Roy to be waiting for her when she finished nearly an hour later, after the girls had showered, changed and cleaned up.

Locking the room, she carried the soccer balls to the equipment area, then headed toward the faculty parking lot. As she stepped from the building and into the darkness of the late afternoon, she saw Roy silhouetted against one of the lights. He'd pulled his vehicle around to where she'd parked and leaned casually against the fender as if he had nothing better to do.

"I wondered if you'd gotten lost in there." He straightened as she approached and moved toward her.

"Hi." His being here flustered her. Roy Fletcher was a very important man, far too important to spend valuable time watching her coach a soccer game. "I thought I saw you." That wasn't the most intelligent comment she'd ever made, but she couldn't think of anything better.

"I didn't get here until halftime."

"You didn't need to come. I certainly didn't expect you to."

"I didn't expect to come, either," he confessed. His hands were plunged deep in his overcoat pockets. "It's been years since I've attended a soccer match. This afternoon, a business associate sent me a report about our overseas sales, and I suddenly started thinking about European soccer."

"They take it very seriously over there."

"Seems to me your girls do, too."

"True." She nodded slowly. "My team works hard and winning is important, but it's about far more than that."

"I disagree," he countered. "Winning is everything."

"Perhaps in your line of work."

"In every line of work. In everything. Look at soccer. Each game is important, right?"

Julie held up her hand. Life and business were intense for Roy. Or maybe life *was* business in his view. "Now isn't the time to be having this conversation," she said briskly. Julie was tired and cold and beyond reasoning with Roy Fletcher. If he wanted to argue, she'd prefer to be at her best, and currently shc was far from it.

"You're right," he murmured as he walked her to her car.

"You came, and I'd like to thank you for that," she said.

"That's the weird part," Roy continued. "I got sidetracked there for a moment. As I said, I was looking at European sales figures, and I started thinking about soccer. Then I remembered that you were coaching a game this afternoon and I had this strange urge to come and watch."

She noticed the urge hadn't been to come and see her. "Strange urge or not, I'm honored you were here." She told herself it was ludicrous to feel disappointed that *she* hadn't been the reason.

"It was an excellent game."

"Thank you on behalf of my team." She inserted the key into her lock, anxious now to get home and under a hot shower.

"And you're an excellent coach."

Again she smiled her appreciation. She tossed her backpack on the passenger seat. She didn't want to be rude by climbing into her car and driving away, but Roy didn't seem to have anything more to say.

As it turned out, Julie was wrong about that.

"Do you enjoy clam chowder?" he asked unexpectedly.

"Yes, I do." It was one of her favorite soups.

"There's a little hole-in-the-wall café not far from here. They used to serve the most incredible clam chowder. I don't even know if the café's still open. I haven't been there in years, but I'm willing to look if you are."

Julie wanted to be sure she understood what he was asking her. "Are you inviting me to dinner?" He seemed nervous about this, but she must be misreading him. Roy Fletcher had nothing to be nervous about.

"Yes, I guess I am asking you to dinner." He brushed a hand across his face. "Like I said, I don't know if the café is still open. I ate there in college quite a lot. The food was cheap and good."

Money certainly wasn't something he needed to worry about now.

The differences between them—between his fame and wealth and her middle-class obscurity—would probably be a factor if they were to continue to see each other. In a flash Julie understood; it was more than dinner he was asking her about. He did want to see her, get to know her, and he was asking if she felt the same way about him.

The look in his eyes was intense. "I like what I know about you, Julie."

She was more than a little shaken. Roy Fletcher was interested in dating *her,* a thirty-year-old teacher with few marriage prospects. "Other than your tendency to be a bit arrogant, I like you, too."

He grinned. "You have your faults."

"Oh, yeah?"

"The word *stubborn* comes to mind."

"I'm stubborn when I happen to be right." She wasn't letting that one pass.

He smiled. "I think that's a conversation we should reserve for another time," he said, echoing her earlier remark. "Agreed?"

She nodded. "I can go to dinner dressed like this?" She had on a nylon blue-and-white running suit—the Abraham Lincoln school colors. Her name was printed across the back with the silkscreen of a wolf, the team symbol.

"Sure," he said. "Why don't you come with me and then I'll drive you back here to pick up your car when we're finished?"

"Sounds good."

Once they were in the neighborhood, it took Roy fifteen minutes to find the café. The restaurant had moved in the eight years since he'd last eaten there. They sat in a booth in a far corner, ordered clam chowder and coffee and discussed movies, politics, the stock market, the state of the economy and a thousand other things. Before she realized it, the café was closing.

As Julie undressed for bed that night, she could hardly believe they'd had so much to talk about. For three hours, they'd chatted nonstop, as if they'd known each other their entire lives. She felt genuinely comfortable with him, enjoying his warmth and wit, qualities she wouldn't have guessed he had a couple of weeks ago. After a quick e-mail to Letty, she got into bed.

If anything surprised her, it was the fact that Roy didn't kiss her when he dropped her off at the school to pick up her car. He wanted to—she was sure of it—and she wanted him to, but…

"Are we still on for tomorrow night?" he'd asked.

Julie was looking forward to it more than ever. "Yes. As far as I'm concerned. What about you?"

"Oh, yes."

That was when she thought he might kiss her. He didn't, but she had the distinct impression he intended to make up for it while they watched the Christmas ships.

CHAPTER FIFTEEN

ANNE FLETCHER strolled leisurely along the Seattle waterfront on her way to Pike Place Market. Julie Wilcoff had agreed to meet her at the seafood stand at noon. Christmas was only two weeks away, and the city was festive with holiday decorations and full of contagious excitement. Even the leaden sky couldn't dampen Anne's spirits. Despite being alone, Anne felt the goodwill and joy of others as they went about their business.

As she walked up the tiered stairway called Hill Climb from the waterfront area to the market, Anne paused to look back over Elliot Bay, watching as the green-and-white Washington State Ferry glided toward the pier. On a clear day she'd be able to see the snow-crested tops of the Olympic Mountains to the east and the Cascade Mountains to the west. Until the divorce, California had been Anne's only home. She'd loved living on the ocean; her daily routine had included long walks on the beach. That was a habit she'd continued when she came to Washington.

The move north had been a financial necessity, as well as a practical choice. Roy lived close by, and while she treasured her independence, she needed the security of having her only child near at hand. It helped that property values were low enough in the more sparsely populated San Juan Islands to allow her to purchase a small cottage. The contentment she derived from her daily walks had rejuvenated her spirits and helped her recover in those first dreadful months after the divorce.

Seattle and the Puget Sound area were beginning to feel like home. Anne wouldn't say she was happy but she wasn't unhappy, either. She'd found satisfaction in her art, and seeing her son fall in love again brought renewed hope for the future.

As Anne made her way through the tide of shoppers and tourists, she discovered Julie waiting for her. The girl was as tall as her father, whom Anne had met the afternoon she'd painted the company window. She'd be a good match for Roy, physically and mentally. She smiled as she recalled her first meeting with Julie, a memory inextricably connected with her painting on the window. The painting had created something of a stir, according to Eleanor Johnson, Roy's assistant. Fletcher Industries employees had reacted to the angels over Bethlehem the same way Marta had responded to her portrait of the angel. Ms. Johnson claimed the artwork on the window was the talk of the building. Everyone loved it, she said. Knowing her art pleased others brought Anne a sense of joy.

''Merry Christmas, Mrs. Fletcher.''

The greeting caught Anne unawares, involved in her thoughts as she was. ''Julie, hello!'' Anne leaned forward to kiss Julie on the cheek. ''Call me Anne, please.''

''All right.''

She slipped her arm through Julie's, and they started walking into the market. ''I can't resist taking a peek, can you?'' The aisles between the vendors' stalls were crowded with customers buying seafood, vegetables and flowers, both fresh and dried. Arts and crafts shops were located downstairs.

''I love it here,'' Julie told her. ''My mother used to bring my sister and me to the market on special occasions when we were little. She'd purchase a fresh salmon just so we could see the young men toss them back and forth.''

''You must have a wonderful mother,'' Anne said.

''I did. She died earlier this year.'' Julie paused as though it was difficult to speak of her mother. ''Dad and I miss her so much.''

Anne gave the girl's arm a gentle squeeze. ''It's more difficult around Christmas, isn't it? Especially the first Christmas.''

Julie nodded. ''Dad and I don't have the tree up yet. We just can't seem to muster the spirit. I'm hoping we can do it this weekend.''

Anne tried to think of a way to introduce Roy into the conversation. ''Roy isn't much for celebrating Christmas. He'll come to my place for the day, but only because he knows I want him to. I think if it was up to him, he'd be just as happy to go to the office and appreciate the fact that he isn't likely to be interrupted.'' It hurt a little to admit that, but it was the truth.

''Ebenezer Scrooge, is he?''

Anne smiled and matched her steps with Julie's. ''Yes, I do believe he is.''

''Oh, my!'' Julie exclaimed, stopping abruptly. ''Did you see that?''

''See what?'' Anne looked around and didn't see anything out of the ordinary.

''A fish just flew!''

''A fish flew,'' Anne repeated, certain she'd misunderstood the other woman. ''These young men throw them back and forth,'' she reminded Julie.

''Yes, I know, but one just took off on its own—no one was standing next to it.'' She hesitated and seemed uncertain. ''I must've missed something. Oh, there goes another one!''

Anne looked at the fresh seafood nestled on a bed of crushed ice. Sure enough, a huge coho salmon was spread across a display of large prawns. Just as she noticed it was out of place, the salmon sprang straight up in the air and started to spin tail over fins, as if someone had actually caught it on a line. Anne rubbed her eyes, convinced she was hallucinating.

''Did you *see* that?'' Julie whispered.

"I did," Anne said. "I think we should get out of here. There's something strange going on."

"I couldn't agree with you more."

Arms linked, the two women walked quickly out of the crowded market. Anne couldn't believe other people hadn't seen this startling phenomenon. But no one else had reacted at all, let alone with awe or astonishment.

Fifteen minutes later, they were in an Italian eatery off a side street. They sat at a small table with a red-checkered tablecloth; a half-melted candle stuck in an empty wine bottle served as the centerpiece. It reminded Anne of the inexpensive restaurants, usually situated in basements, that she and Burton used to frequent when he was in law school.... She cast off the nostalgia before it could trap her.

Anne and Julie both ordered a glass of Chianti with their spinach salads.

"I'm seeing Roy again tonight," Julie said after her first sip of wine. "We...had dinner last night."

"*And* on Wednesday and Thursday." Anne had discovered this quite by accident when she'd phoned the house to arrange her luncheon date with Julie. It had given Anne such hope, such encouragement. Julie had made a point of letting her know that her father had invited him on Thursday—but that didn't explain Wednesday. Or Friday.

"We talked for a long time last night."

Anne noticed that Julie's hand tightened around

the stem of her wineglass. She had to restrain herself from leaping up and shouting for joy. She wondered how much of their story Julie knew, so she asked, "Did he mention Aimee?"

Julie's eyes held hers. "No. Is she the reason you suggested lunch?"

"Not really." Anne shrugged. "I hope you don't think I'm a busybody."

"Of course not."

"I'm so pleased Roy's finally met someone he can love." Julie abruptly dropped her gaze and Anne realized she'd spoken out of turn. "Oh, dear, forgive me. I shouldn't have said that."

"I don't know if Roy loves me—and it's certainly too soon to know how I feel about him."

"I'm so sorry. Please forget I said anything. I'm just a meddling old woman who's eager for grandchildren." The instant the words were out of her mouth, Anne realized she'd done it again.

"Grandchildren?" Julie's eyes grew huge.

"Oh, dear," Anne gasped. "I do seem to be having trouble keeping my foot out of my mouth." She set her wineglass down, determined not to take another sip until she'd fully recovered from whatever had loosened her tongue. Every word out of her mouth embarrassed her more.

"I take it Roy was once in love with Aimee," Julie said as the waiter brought their salads.

"He wanted to marry her, but she chose…

someone else.'' Anne hoped to avoid the more sordid details.

''Seeing how successful Roy is now, I imagine she's sorry.'' Suddenly Julie looked chagrinned and she lowered her fork. ''Forgive me. That was a dreadful thing to suggest.''

Immersed in her own thoughts, Anne was confused. ''Dreadful? How?''

''I didn't mean to imply that the only reason Aimee or any woman would love Roy is because he's successful.''

''I know you didn't mean anything disparaging,'' Anne assured her. ''Besides, you're wrong.''

Julie looked puzzled, and Anne felt obliged to explain the situation. ''Aimee doesn't appear to have any regrets.''

''Then she's happy?''

''I wouldn't know. You see—'' Anne took a deep breath ''—she's married to my husband.'' Although she tried hard to keep her emotions out of it, Anne heard the hint of bitterness in her voice and swallowed down the lump that formed in her throat. ''Forgive me, Julie, I meant my ex-husband.''

The linen napkin on Julie's lap slipped unnoticed to the floor. ''No wonder Roy has a problem with trust,'' she murmured. ''His fiancée, his father…''

''Now you know,'' Anne said softly. ''Roy wouldn't appreciate my telling you, though.''

''I won't say a word.''

Anne appreciated that. ''Actually, digging up the

skeletons in our family's sad history isn't why I asked you to lunch,'' Anne confessed. ''I want to get to know you better.''

''I feel the same way. I loved the picture you painted on the window. Dad says everyone's talking about it, and Roy speaks so fondly of you and—''

''What did he say?''

''Well,'' Julie said, beaming Anne a bright smile, ''he brags about you.''

''My son brags about me?'' Anne hated to sound like an echo, but she was shocked. Half the time, she felt as though she was nothing more than an obligation in her son's life. He only tolerated her concern and seldom sought out her company.

''He's very impressed with your work. He told me about several of your pieces he's displayed in the building. He promised to show them to me on my next visit.''

''If you can get in,'' Anne teased. It'd been a source of amusement, the trouble Julie had getting past the security guard.

''Ah, yes, Jason, protector of the gate.'' Julie rolled her eyes.

Anne had witnessed for herself how determined the young man was to keep poor Julie on the other side of the company doors. She stabbed at a piece of spinach. ''Let me make sure I understood you correctly. Did you really say Roy has my artwork hanging in his office building?''

''That's what he told me.''

This was news.

"Five landscapes, I think he said. You didn't know that?"

Anne shook her head. "I never told him my pseudonym."

"He must've found it out on his own," Julie said evenly.

"I...I don't know what to say. Part of me is pleased and another part is irritated."

"But why? He's proud of your talent."

"I've told him a dozen times that I refuse to let him support me. I want my paintings to sell on their own merit. The last thing I want or need, especially from my own son, is charity."

"I doubt Roy would display work he didn't sincerely admire, especially in his own building."

Julie meant she was overreacting, Anne thought. "You're right of course." To cover her embarrassment, she dug into her salad.

Julie reached for a warm sourdough roll. "I'm glad you asked me to lunch."

"As I said, I want to get to know you better—and I want to thank you for being so patient with my son."

Julie lowered her head and struggled to hide a grin. "We've certainly had our ups and downs. He's surprised me more than once."

Anne found this curious. "In what way?"

"Dinner on Thursday night—to take one example. I made a pot of black-bean soup and he seemed to really enjoy it. Plain ol' black-bean soup.''

''You cook?''

Julie nodded. ''A little. My twin sister is the real chef in the family, but I'm learning.''

''Are you close to your sister?''

''Very. She lives in Florida, but we talk almost every day via e-mail. I've told her about Roy.'' Julie glanced down, as if she regretted telling Anne that.

Anne struggled unsuccessfully to keep her tears at bay.

''Anne, is everything all right?'' Julie leaned across the table and squeezed her hand.

''Of course it is,'' Anne whispered, smiling through her tears. ''It's just that I'm so glad.... I'd given up hope, you see. I'd convinced myself that Roy had completely closed himself off from love, and now he's met you and the whole world looks brighter. Thank you, Julie, thank you so much.''

Julie shook her head. ''You don't have anything to thank me for.''

''But I do,'' Anne countered. ''Don't you see, my dear Julie? You are the answer to my prayers.''

CHAPTER SIXTEEN

THE CATERER'S STAFF delivered dinner and skillfully set the dining room table in his condo, adding candles and flowers to create a romantic mood. Before they left, Roy paid them handsomely and inspected their work, admiring the small touches.

He'd been looking forward to this evening with Julie all day. He'd longed to kiss her the night before and hadn't. He berated himself for the missed opportunity. He'd sensed the disappointment in her and felt it himself. But he wanted more than kisses—he yearned to make love to her.

He hadn't experienced these primal emotions, these deep erotic urges, in years. They were little more than a distant memory now. But with Julie…

The table was covered with an off-white linen cloth that had an elegant gold edging. It wouldn't have been his choice, but the caterer had brought it with her. A large candle inside a glass hurricane lamp, surrounded by poinsettias and sprigs of holly, adorned the center of the table. Again, that had been part of the dinner package. When he'd explained his requirements to Ms. Johnson and the caterer's staff, he'd been assured that they'd be able to create the mood he desired. His trust had been well-placed; his home had never looked better.

Everything about the condo spoke of romance. The lights were dimmed and lit candles were arranged in strategic spots around the room. In the background, Christmas carols played softly. The stage was set. Roy, dressed in dark slacks and a gray cashmere sweater, checked his watch. Julie was due any minute.

While he waited, he poured himself a glass of chardonnay. To his surprise, he was nervous. He couldn't imagine why—or could he? His mind flitted from the past to the present and back again. The past was painful and the present was unpredictable…and the future? Well, who knew about the future?

Initially this relationship hadn't been too promising, but it had gained momentum in the past few days. Even now he wasn't entirely convinced that Julie was for real, that the settlement offer truly didn't interest her.

Gradually Roy could feel himself being drawn toward her, almost against his will. He'd decided never to fall in love again, but Julie Wilcoff made him crave the experience of love, the sensations and the feelings and the *hope.* This sense of wanting to be part of life again frightened him a little; so did the eagerness that surged through him at the prospect. Love eventually brought pain and betrayal. Yet all day he'd thought of little else but this dinner with Julie and the kisses they were bound to share.

His phone rang and he reached for the receiver, already knowing it was her. "Hello."

"I'm here." Even the sound of her voice was sultry and sexy.

He hit the numbers that automatically opened the electronic gates to grant her entrance. He couldn't resist taking his private elevator to the lobby so he could escort her up to his suite.

Standing by the glass doors that marked the entry into the beautifully decorated lobby, Roy watched as Julie walked from her car to the building. Her head was bent against the cold. She had on a long wool coat, which she'd left unbuttoned. Beneath it, he noticed the black skirt and matching jacket with a frilly white blouse. He was struck by her loveliness. Every time he saw her, she seemed to look more beautiful. Was that just a matter of perception or was he finally seeing what had always been there?

He held open the door and stepped back to let her enter. Once she was inside, he made a long, leisurely appraisal and sucked in his breath. Only one word came to mind. "Wow!"

"You like?" Holding open her coat, she slowly rotated to give him a better look.

"I like a lot."

"Don't act so surprised," she muttered. "I clean up good."

"I'll say." With his hand at her elbow, he steered

her toward the elevator, which took them directly to the suite, the doors opening into his living room, with the large picture windows that overlooked Lake Washington. He'd grown accustomed to the spectacular sight and it no longer astonished him as it once had. But the view captured Julie's attention the instant she stepped out of the elevator. An uninterrupted panorama of Lake Washington and the sparkling Seattle lights stretched before her like some kind of Christmas fantasy.

"Oh, Roy," she whispered, "this takes my breath away."

"It's what sold me on the place." To his chagrin, she remained rooted to the spot. Seemingly without her noticing, he removed her coat, one sleeve at a time, and hung it in the hall closet. When he returned, she still hadn't moved.

"The parade of ships is supposed to start in less than thirty minutes."

She walked close to the window and, standing next to her, Roy pointed out some of the sights. "Naturally, the view is even more spectacular in daylight," he said.

"I can hardly imagine anything more beautiful than this." She hadn't even glanced around his condo, but Roy didn't care. Although it was a showpiece, he rarely had anyone up to visit. He'd heard that people were curious about his home, but Julie was obviously more intrigued by the view.

Without asking, Roy poured her a glass of wine.

Joining her once again, he handed it to her. "Shall we have a glass of wine before we eat?"

"Thank you." She accepted the glass, then turned back to stare out the window. "I can't bear to look away. This is just so beautiful."

He'd thought he'd wait to kiss her, but realized that delaying it a moment longer was beyond him. Taking the wineglass from her hand, placing it on the wide windowsill, he gently turned her toward him. "What you need is a distraction."

He didn't know a woman of thirty could blush, but blush she did. For long seconds her eyes searched his, telling him she wanted his kiss.

Bringing her into his arms, he watched as her eyes drifted closed and she leaned into his embrace. Then they were kissing with the familiarity and ease of longtime lovers. Roy felt a small tremor go through her, or perhaps he was the one who trembled; he no longer knew. What he did know was how *good* it felt to hold her.

She was taller than any other women he'd kissed, broader through the shoulders, too, but he liked that. In fact, he liked everything about Julie. When she kissed him back, he realized he liked her sweet, slightly exotic taste. He immediately wanted to kiss her again. She opened to him a little more, parting her lips, as her arms eased upward and wound around his neck.

A voice in his mind started shouting that kissing her was too damned wonderful to continue without consequences. He hadn't intended to let things go this far, this fast, but there was no stopping either of them. Not yet. A few more kisses and then he'd pull away and they could go back to enjoying their wine.

Another kiss. Then he'd stop. Then he'd pause long enough to clear his head.

But already his hands, which had been innocently stroking her back, had worked their way down her waist. He loved the feel of her, loved the gentle contours of her utterly feminine body. As their kissing went on, it was hard to keep from touching more and more of her.

It'd been a long time since anything had felt so good.

"Nice," he whispered, reluctantly easing his mouth from hers. He could barely think, barely focus on anything but the woman in his arms.

"Very nice," she whispered.

Their eyes held. Her hands remained on his shoulders and his stayed on her waist. "Are you ready for dinner?"

She gave him the softest smile. "No." Her voice was a mere wisp of sound.

"Me, neither." He kissed her again, his mouth coaxing hers. Her lips were pliant, warm, moist. He didn't know how long they went on like that, lost in each other.

"Julie, listen..." Even to his own ears his voice was hoarse. He braced his forehead against hers.

"I'm listening."

"We're getting a little hot and heavy here."

"Yes…I'd noticed." She kissed the side of his neck and shivers raced down his spine.

"You don't have to be so agreeable."

He splayed his fingers through her hair, thinking that would bring her to her senses. In his experience, women didn't want their hair disheveled. Julie barely seemed aware of it. He should have known….

He purposely pulled away, thinking that too much of a good thing would soon bore him. But he wasn't bored. Julie had the opposite effect on him, just as she had from the first.

"Dinner's about ready." Superhuman effort allowed him to drop his arms and step back from her. Julie reached for her wineglass and Roy saw that her hands trembled.

He took a few moments to regain his composure in the kitchen. Dinner, a chicken dish—he couldn't remember what the caterer had called it—was warming in the oven. The salad sat on the top shelf of the refrigerator. Roy opened the door and stood directly in the blast of cold air with his eyes closed, hoping it would shock him into reality.

"It looks like the parade is about to start," Julie called from the other room.

Roy grinned. She was at the window again. "I'll be a couple of minutes."

"Don't rush on my account."

The meal now seemed a necessary nuisance. The

truth was, Roy had no appetite for anything but Julie. For days he'd been conscious of how badly he wanted to kiss her, but he hadn't known what to expect once he did.

"Can I do anything to help?" Julie asked, coming into the kitchen. She sounded far more like herself.

"Not a thing. All I have to do is bring these dishes into the dining room." He carried the salad out and set it on the table.

Julie walked over to the fireplace and once again her back was to him. "Your home is lovely."

"Would you like a tour before we eat?"

She turned around, then surprised him by shaking her head. "I'm afraid we might not make it out of the bedroom."

Roy had always found her honesty refreshing and never more than at that moment. He chuckled. "I'm feeling the same way myself."

"I...we haven't known each other long enough for that kind of commitment."

Now, *that* was a word Roy went out of his way to avoid. Instead of commenting, he chose to ignore it. "The salad is served." He stood behind her chair and held it for her.

Once Julie was seated, he took his own place across from her; they both had a full view of the parade of Christmas ships as they sailed or motored past. Julie remarked every now and then on a certain theme or design. After a second glass of wine, she declined another.

Rejecting caution, Roy poured himself a third. He needed something to fortify him if he was going to battle temptation. And Julie tempted him, all right. It wasn't easy to admit that, since Roy was a man who enjoyed being in control. And yet all through dinner—the chicken-and-mushroom dish, new potatoes and sautéed spinach—it wasn't the food so expertly prepared or even their conversation that engaged him. No, what was foremost in Roy's mind was the desire he felt for Julie. This weakness distressed him and at the same time, he hadn't felt so alive in years.

"Dessert?" Julie asked.

The question startled Roy and he suddenly realized she'd carried the dinner plates into the kitchen and returned with two dessert plates. Cheesecake, if he recalled correctly.

"No." For emphasis he shook his head. "On second thought…" He caught her around the waist and pulled her onto his lap.

She set the plates on the table, her face close to his. Her eyes, dark and intense, were wide and so very expressive. They told him she wanted to kiss him again. Her throat was flushed, her skin warm. If *her* feelings were this easy to decipher, he could only imagine what she could read in *his* face.

"We're supposed to be watching the ships, remember?" Her voice trembled.

"I know."

She sighed and asked, ''What's happening to us?''

Roy knew, but he didn't like the answer any more than he welcomed the question. ''I don't think we need to figure that out just yet.''

''My head's spinning—and it doesn't have anything to do with the wine.''

''Mine, too,'' he told her. The alcohol was only partially responsible for the dizziness he was feeling. He could envision himself poised above Julie, ready to slowly sink his body into hers...slowly be enveloped in her warmth.

''I...I saw a fish fly this afternoon,'' she whispered. Her mouth was close to his ear.

Roy frowned, not understanding.

''It's true,'' she said, her voice still low. ''I was at the Pike Place Market, and it seemed to leap off the crushed ice and fly of its own accord.''

''That isn't possible,'' Roy said impatiently. Either it was a trick of the eye or sleight of hand.

''That's what I thought,'' Julie told him. ''Then it happened again and someone else saw it, too.''

''My guess is there's a reason you're telling me this.''

In response, she kissed the side of his neck. ''The way I feel now is the same way I felt earlier when I saw that fish fly. I didn't believe it, although I saw it with my own eyes. I felt a little ridiculous. And I wanted to deny it, pretend it hadn't happened. Then, as I said, someone else confirmed what I'd seen and I realized I hadn't imagined it, after all.''

''So...'' Perhaps it was the scent of her perfume that clogged his brain. But for the life of him, Roy didn't know what she was talking about or where this rather unusual story was taking him.

''I left quickly because I had to get away to think about it.''

Ah, Roy was beginning to understand, and his hold on her tightened. ''You want to leave?''

''I should.''

''What if I asked you to stay?'' Now he was the one kissing her, dropping light kisses along the side of her neck, hoping to lure her into spending the night. She was in his arms, and he was reluctant to let her go. They were both adults who knew what they wanted. He wasn't interested in pretending otherwise. Julie was smart enough to recognize what he was after and admit she wanted it, too.

Her answer was a long time in coming and held a pleading quality. ''Don't ask.''

''All right.'' Difficult as it was, he relaxed his grip.

She stood up from his lap and Roy immediately missed the closeness. He got to his feet, ready to protest when she retrieved her coat from the closet.

''I don't want you to go.''

She smiled, walked over to where he stood and kissed him on the mouth. ''I don't want to go, either.''

"Then stay." He bit his tongue before he made the mistake of saying more. This decision had to be hers.

For just a moment, Roy thought he'd succeeded, but then he watched a renewed determination settle over her. "I can't. I just saw a fish fly through the air."

He didn't know what it was about that stupid fish, but it appeared to have some significance for her.

"I can't quite believe what's happened," she said, "but I'm afraid I'm falling in love with you."

Love? Roy's heart fell. That was the last thing he wanted to hear.

CHAPTER SEVENTEEN

JULIE STEPPED BACK from the freshly cut Christmas tree her father had begrudgingly set up in a corner of the living room. This was probably the most difficult part of the Christmas season for him.

And for her.

Her mother had particularly loved their little tree-trimming ceremony. Just a year ago, the three of them had decorated the tree together. Andy Williams's Christmas album had played in the background, as it always did, and the smell of popped corn had permeated the air.

''It's perfect,'' Julie announced.

Her father shrugged. ''If you say so. I brought the decorations up from the basement.'' He studied the tree, and Julie had the feeling that if she hadn't made the effort this year, he'd be willing to forgo Christmas altogether.

''Did you find the Christmas CDs?'' she asked.

''Nope.''

Julie suspected he hadn't looked. The CDs were probably packed away with the decorations.

''I think I'll see how the Huskies are doing.'' He

reached for the remote. The University of Washington football team was her father's favorite.

"You aren't going to help decorate?" Julie hated the thought of doing it all by herself, but she didn't want to force her father to participate. Lectures from her wouldn't help, as Letty's e-mail had reminded her that morning.

Her father's eyes grew sad. "I'm sorry, Kitten, but I just don't have the heart for it this year."

He hardly ever called her Kitten, a name from her childhood, and she blinked away tears. After everything they'd endured, Julie couldn't complain about his unwillingness to take part in an activity that brought back memories he might not be ready to face. "That's okay," she told him, although her heart was breaking. This was hard, so much harder than she'd known it would be.

"I can do it," Julie said more to convince herself than her father. Maybe it wouldn't be as painful if he stayed in the room. "You can be my adviser."

He acquiesced with a reluctant nod. Settling down in his usual chair, he clicked the remote and after flipping through several channels, came upon the Huskies game.

Humming "Deck the Halls" to herself, Julie located the string of lights and began to weave it around the base of the evergreen, working her way upward. This task was usually reserved for her father. Afterward, Julie and Letty—before her twin sister married—along with their mother, took over the task of hanging the decorations. It had been an important tradition, representing a time of family fun, laughter and music. Now it seemed bleak and sad....

"Did you check those lights before you started putting them on the tree?" her father asked during the first commercial break.

"Uh..."

"I can see that you didn't." He clambered out of his chair. "Oh, all right, I'll do the lights, but that's it."

"Thanks, Dad!"

"I should've known," he muttered. "All you wanted me to do was put up the tree, you said. Well, I did that. Next thing you know, I'm stringing the lights. Are you plotting against me?"

"Would I do that?" she asked in a singsong voice that didn't conceal her amusement.

Since there wasn't much she could do while he strung the lights, Julie went into the kitchen and put a package of popcorn in the microwave. It was cheating, she supposed; her mother had done it the old-fashioned way. Still, popcorn was popcorn.

"If you're going to be popping corn, I want the buttered kind."

"Yes, Dad."

He was almost finished with the lights by the time she returned to the living room, carrying a large bowl filled to overflowing with popcorn. She set it in the center of the coffee table and got down on all fours to sort through the boxes he'd brought up from the basement.

"I'll probably be putting up ornaments, too," her father grumbled. He paused long enough to reach for a handful of popcorn. "Did I ever tell you about Christmas the first year your mother and I were married? We were too poor to afford a tree. A friend gave your mother a poinsettia, and we put our gifts under that." He smiled at the memory. "It was the most pitiful-looking thing, but you'd have thought it was as grand as a fifteen-foot tree."

Of all the gifts Julie had received through the years, perhaps the best was the fact that her parents had loved each other deeply.

"What I remember was all of us attending Christmas Eve services and then coming home and opening one gift each." Julie and Letty were eight years old before they realized that the one gift they were allowed to open always turned out to be pajamas.

"I'm going to miss Mom's turkey stuffing," Julie said, sitting back on her heels. For both Thanksgiving and Christmas, her mother had prepared the traditional turkey. Every year she fretted over her stuffing and every year she outdid herself.

"Yours wasn't bad," her father assured her.

Like her mother, Julie had worried excessively over her first attempt at cooking the Thanksgiving turkey. "Thanks, Dad. I guess I must've picked up something all those years I spent helping Mom." It felt good to be able to talk freely about her mother.

Her father seemed to revel in it, too, although she knew he'd felt wary about reliving the past. Sharing memories made missing her less painful, and Julie knew that these memories would get them through the Christmas season. There would be poignant, tearful moments, but happy ones, too.

"Are you cooking a turkey for Christmas?" her father asked.

Julie hadn't given the matter much thought. Christmas was still two weeks away, and it seemed a bit early to be thinking about what she'd serve. "I suppose."

"Seems to me we had leftover turkey for at least a week after Thanksgiving."

Julie took out the ornaments, examining each one. "Would you rather I cooked something else?"

"No, no, I like my turkey. It just seems a waste to buy a big bird for the two of us."

"I could find a smaller one."

"Or...maybe we should invite a few guests."

"Guests? Who?" All their family was on the East Coast. Letty was in Florida, and longtime friends had their own families.

"I was thinking of Roy and his mother."

He'd led into that suggestion with such ease Julie hadn't seen it coming. For a moment, she was too surprised to respond.

"What do you think?" he asked, watching her.

"Well," she said cautiously, "I don't know."

Her father brought the stepladder from the kitchen

as he continued his task. ''I met Anne this week, and she's a sensible woman.''

Julie had liked Roy's mother immensely—and she'd been given real insight into Anne's son. On Saturday evening, she'd gone to his home with a new awareness of him, an appreciation for the man he was. Consequently her guard had been down. She'd felt as if her heart would shatter with joy when he kissed her. More than that, she'd sensed there could be a profound connection between them. But she had no way of knowing if Roy felt the same things she did. She *believed* he did, but that could be just wishful thinking.

''You're not saying anything.'' Her father frowned at her over the top of his reading glasses as he stood on the stepladder by the tree.

''That might be nice, but I don't know if they'll accept.''

''It won't do any harm to ask.''

She agreed. This suggestion was unlike her father—but then it dawned on Julie that he might be saying something else. ''You like Mrs. Fletcher, Dad?'' It was logical; after all, he was alone, and so was Roy's mother.

Her father paused, the string of lights dangling between his hands. ''I know what you're thinking, Julie.''

''Dad, Mrs. Fletcher is a wonderful woman.''

''I'm sure she is, but I want to make something clear right now, and this is important. Anne Fletcher would never interest me romantically. No woman could replace your mother.''

''Dad, I didn't mean—''

''I know you didn't,'' he said, cutting her off. ''But it's best to let you know that I don't plan to remarry, ever. I loved your mother, and frankly, there's no room in my heart for anyone else.''

''You might feel differently down the road. Mom wouldn't want you to be lonely.''

''I won't be. I have every intention of working as long as I can and living a productive life.''

''I certainly hope so,'' she teased.

''But I'll live the rest of my life alone.''

''That decision is yours.''

''I appreciate your understanding. At some point, you and your sister might feel inclined to match me up, but I'm telling you, it's not what I want.''

''All right, Dad.''

He nodded, apparently relieved.

Julie scooped up a handful of popcorn and had just started to chew when her father glanced up again. ''You were home earlier than I expected last night. Was everything okay between you and Roy?''

She swallowed quickly. ''It went really well.''

''Are you going out with him again?''

Roy hadn't asked, but she'd come to the conclusion that he would. ''I think so,'' and then she added, because it was true, ''I hope so. Does that bother you?''

Her father grinned. ''It's a little late to be asking me that, don't you think?''

''Yeah, I suppose it is. I like him, Dad.''

Her father's grin broadened. ''I guessed as much. You've been walking on air for the last few days.''

''Is it that noticeable?''

Her father chuckled and was about to say something else when the doorbell rang.

Julie stood, brushed off her jeans and hurried to the door. Roy Fletcher stood on the other side. A surge of joy washed through her at the sight of him.

''Hi,'' he said a bit sheepishly.

''Hi, yourself.''

''You doing anything special?''

She nodded and reached for his hand, pulling him into the foyer. ''Want to help?''

''Maybe.'' He wrapped his arms around her waist. Nuzzling her neck with his cold nose, he whispered, ''I woke up this morning and realized I missed you. By the way—'' he dropped a kiss on her forehead ''—I bought tickets for a Christmas concert, if you're interested.''

''I'd love it.'' Happy chills raced down Julie's back and she sighed as he kissed her jaw, working his way toward her lips. They were deeply involved in a kiss when Julie heard her father behind her.

''Yup,'' he said gleefully. ''I'd say my Julie likes Mr. Roy Fletcher.''

''I'D SAY SHE DOES, too,'' Mercy shouted, and exchanged a high five with Goodness. ''Just look at the two of them.''

Frowning, Shirley stood back, arms crossed. "It was too easy."

"What do you mean?" Mercy demanded. "I don't know about you, but I've been working hard to bring these two humans together. And I think I did a very good job."

Shirley shook her head. "Trouble's in the making, I can feel it. I'm telling you something's going to happen that none of us will like."

"Well, don't go looking for it," Goodness warned.

"I'm not," the oldest of the trio insisted, "but I can sense it coming."

"Don't say that," Mercy cried, covering both ears. "Roy and Julie are *perfect* together. They're falling in love, just the way we planned."

"I wish I could agree," Shirley said. "But experience tells me it was just too easy. Mark my words, they're about to hit a major snag."

"You're just upset about that salmon," Mercy pouted.

Goodness wasn't thrilled about the fish free-for-all in Pike Place Market, but any chastisement would only encourage Mercy to misbehave. After Julie and Anne had left, Mercy had gone amuck. Fish had been flying in all directions. Staff and customers were shouting and shrieking; chaos was rampant. It'd taken both Shirley and Goodness to get her out of the fish market.

''What could go wrong?'' Goodness asked.

''Yes, just look at them,'' Mercy said. Roy and Julie had started to place the ornaments on the tree. Between each carefully hung bauble, they'd pause and exchange kisses and munch popcorn. ''He's even telling her about Christmases he had as a boy. We all know he doesn't often talk about his parents.''

''Speaking of parents,'' Goodness said, looking around. ''Where's Dean?''

''He made an excuse to leave and give them privacy.''

''That's very considerate.''

Shirley continued to frown. ''I wish I had a better feeling about all of this.''

So did Goodness, but she'd come to respect her friend's premonitions. She could only wonder what would happen next.

CHAPTER EIGHTEEN

IT WAS BEGINNING to look and feel like Christmas, Anne thought as she walked out to her rural mailbox. The neighbors, whose house could barely be seen in the distance, had strung a multicolored strand of outside lights along their roofline. A six-foot-tall Frosty the Snowman stood forlornly in their front yard. Snow was a rare commodity in the Pacific Northwest, and a fake snowman was all there was likely to be.

As Anne strolled back up the meandering driveway that led to her cottage, she looked through the assortment of holiday cards, bills and sale flyers. She'd been so busy with her artwork and traveling into Seattle that the mail had sat forgotten in her box for three days. Pouring herself a cup of tea, Anne settled at the small round table in her cozy kitchen and opened the top envelope.

It was clearly a Christmas card, an expensive one, with the return address embossed in gold on the back of the envelope. Anne opened it and slid out the thick card. The scene was of snow and geese and a decorated Christmas tree in the middle of a pristine meadow. Curious now, she opened it and gasped as she read the embossed name. A sharp pain slashed through her and she held her breath, closing her eyes at such blatant cruelty.

Burton and Aimee Fletcher

This Christmas card was obviously Burton's way of reminding Anne of what he'd done to her. Not that she needed reminders… She didn't know why her ex-husband hated her so much. Perhaps it was because, thanks to Aimee and the divorce, Burton had lost his son. Was he blaming *her* for that?

Refusing to dwell on the reasons for such unkindness, she tossed the card aside and reached for the rest of her mail. Her hands shook as she struggled to regain her composure. How sad that five years after their divorce, her ex-husband was still trying to upset her. Well, Anne refused to let him. Then it occurred to her that perhaps it hadn't been Burton at all, but Aimee. If so, Anne couldn't begin to figure out why the other woman would want to hurt her.

Although she tried not to let the Christmas card bother her, Anne couldn't stop thinking about it. The fact that she hadn't recognized the return address told her Burton and Aimee had moved from the oceanfront home Anne had loved so much. She could just imagine the new house. No expense would have been spared; Burton was all too willing to spend his money on Aimee. It thrilled him to have a beautiful young woman on his arm. A woman dressed in designer clothes, wearing lavish jewelry that spoke of her husband's success. He'd done exceptionally well over the years. Twice now, she'd heard his name in conjunction with famous Hollywood stars and their very public divorces.

The phone rang. Anne wasn't in the mood to talk, and decided to let the answering machine pick up the call. Out of curiosity, she glanced at the caller ID. When she saw it was Marta's New York number, she jerked up the receiver.

Anne had been waiting anxiously ever since their last conversation. The temptation to contact her had been almost overwhelming, but she hadn't given in. If Marta had sold the angel painting or wanted to discuss her marriage, she would have called.

''Hi, Marta,'' Anne said, rushing her words together.

''Merry Christmas, Anne.''

Anne so wanted this to be good news. She *needed* it after that dreadful Christmas card.

''How are you?'' Anne asked.

Marta hesitated. ''Good, I think. Do you have a few minutes?''

''Of course I do.'' From the tone of her friend's voice Anne suspected the call had to do with Marta's husband and not the painting.

Marta sighed, a despairing sound. ''I confronted Jack. I tried to follow your advice and casually mention that I knew about the affair. Unfortunately it didn't work. I came unglued.''

''What happened?'' Anne asked softly.

''You suggested I simply tell Jack I knew what he was doing and that I was protecting myself financially. That seemed so reasonable at the time, and I thought I could do it. I really did. But when the moment came, I burst into tears and called him every foul name in the book. I don't think I've ever been so angry. I've never been one to say those kinds of things.''

''This is your life and your marriage, and your heart's breaking.'' Anne had struggled with this same vicious anger herself. Her self-esteem had been shattered; she'd come to the end of her composure, no longer the complacent wife. Her self-recrimination had been as bitter as her resentment and her fury.

''I had no idea I was so furious.''

''I didn't, either, when it happened to me,'' Anne consoled her. She hadn't turned on Burton, though. Instead, she wept until there were no more tears left and all that remained was her anger.

''On the other hand,'' Marta said with high-strained cheerfulness, ''I took your advice and had everything planned before I spoke to him.''

''Good!''

''I saw an attorney and had our joint assets frozen right away.''

Anne approved. ''That was smart—and practical.''

''My attorney advised me to wait a week until he had everything in place. Then Jack came home smelling of her perfume and I went ballistic.''

This was so unlike Marta that Anne could scarcely imagine her friend in such a state. ''How did he react?''

Marta's laugh was short. ''Of course he denied everything.''

As Burton had, accusing Anne of having a filthy mind, of being insecure and ridiculous. In the beginning, she'd felt dreadful for having suspected such terrible things about her husband. Burton had insisted on an apology and in her innocence, Anne had given him one. Her face burned with mortification at the memory.

''Burton denied everything, too.''

''Then I told him about seeing an attorney,'' Marta said, her voice trembling, ''and…and then I threw him out.''

In every likelihood, Jack had immediately gone to the other woman, but Anne didn't mention that.

''He…he didn't want to leave. He kept trying to reason with me but I refused to listen. He said I was imagining things—and this is the crazy part—for a moment I actually believed him. Here he was, hours late, smelling of perfume and denying everything, and because I so badly wanted to believe him, I…I almost did.''

"Of course you wanted to believe him. Jack's your husband."

Marta paused. "That first night was so dreadful. Jack called the apartment ten times. I wouldn't answer the phone and he left messages for me, pleading with me to hear him out." She released a soft hiccuping sob.

"When was that?"

"Three days ago."

"How long has it been since you talked to him?"

"Since that night… I just can't. I thought maybe I'd blown everything out of proportion and, Anne, I'm no longer sure what to believe. I know he's involved with someone else, but I so badly want him back that I've decided I can't trust my own feelings in the matter. If I talk to him, I'm afraid he'll manage to convince me that all of this is nonsense and I'll take him back."

"What are you going to do?"

"Right now, nothing. I hired a private investigator. It sounds so stupid, so cliché. You're the only woman in the world I'd admit this to, but I'm paying a man outrageous fees to follow my husband around and photograph him with another woman. Is that sick or what?"

"Oh, Marta. Of course it isn't. A detective might be the only means you have of learning the truth." Early on, before the breakup of her own marriage, Anne had considered the same thing. In retrospect she wished she'd done it. Photographic evidence might have opened her eyes to what Burton was doing.

"All I want is for this to go away. I think now I should've waited until after Christmas, but Anne, I couldn't. I couldn't endure this another moment. I couldn't pretend and look the other way anymore."

"I'm so sorry, Marta," Anne told her friend. "I wouldn't have wished this on you for anything."

"Oh, Anne, I don't know what to do. Christmas is only a week away. I can't deal with this and the holidays, too. What am I going to tell our friends? How can I possibly face everyone?" The questions came between deep sobs.

"Oh, Marta, I'm so sorry," she said again.

"Why is this happening to me?"

Anne had asked herself the same question hundreds of times. "Would you like to fly out to Seattle? Stay with me and take a few days to collect your thoughts. Let your attorney know you're coming and just get on a plane."

"I can't believe you'd do that for me," Marta said, and continued to sob.

"I've walked in your shoes. I know how hard this is. What do you want to do?"

"Would you mind terribly coming to New York? I'd pay for your ticket. I just need someone with me—someone who understands."

"Of course I wouldn't mind! I'll check on flights the minute we get off the phone." Roy wouldn't care; Anne was sure of that. Her son would be just as happy to spend Christmas Day at Julie's. With Anne in New York, he'd be free to do so.

"Thank you. Oh, thank you, Anne. I'd fly out and join you, but I don't want to leave. There's no telling what Jack would do if I were to vacate the house."

Naturally her friend was right. "That's fine, Marta. I'll come to New York for Christmas and be your moral support."

"Thank you," her friend whispered again. "I don't know how I'd cope if it wasn't for you."

"We'll have a wonderful Christmas," Anne tried to assure her, although she knew what Marta was experiencing. The pain and shock…

"Oh, Anne, I just can't believe Jack would be so stupid."

"He might come to his senses yet."

"I'm not counting on it," Marta said. "He seemed so sincere, so horrified. He kept insisting I was wrong. I never knew he was capable of such lies."

It hurt just to listen to her friend's agony. Anne didn't have the heart to tell her that the pain, even when dulled by time, had a way of resurfacing when you least expected it. Anne had felt its sting only moments earlier when she'd opened her mail.

Marta grew quiet, as if she was composing herself. She took a deep, audible breath. "I've been so caught up in my own troubles I forgot to mention what's been happening with your painting."

Although she was dying to know, Anne was willing to put it off. "That's not important now."

"But it is."

"Did Mrs. Gould decide against it?" Anne asked. She'd never been comfortable with letting the buyer assume she had no intention of selling her angel.

"No, she's more interested than ever, but now there's another prospective buyer."

"That's wonderful," Anne said excitedly.

"This one claims she'll match or beat anything Mrs. Gould offers."

"Are you saying that two customers have gotten into a bidding war?" Anne was almost afraid to guess what this could mean financially.

"That's exactly what I'm saying."

"How...how much?"

"Are you sure you want to know?"

"Yes!" she cried. "Tell me."

"Well, first of all," Marta teased. "I'm not sure the artist would be willing to sell it."

"Oh, Marta." Anne couldn't help it; she giggled.

"It's an incredible painting, and everyone who sees it is drawn to it. Your angel has become the most talked-about piece in our gallery. She's aroused more interest than anything else on display, and of course, the fact that it's December helps. You couldn't have painted her at a more appropriate time."

Anne's heart swelled with pride. "Oh, you make me feel so good!"

"That's what the painting does, you know. People look at your angel and they feel better about life."

"Has she helped you?" Anne asked.

"Oh, yes," Marta replied. "I don't know what it is, but there's a soothing quality about seeing your angel. It's...almost as if I were standing close to God."

Anne regretted having given the angel up so quickly. Even now, she didn't know if she'd imagined the vision or it had actually happened. She chose to believe the angel had been real, but who was to know?

"Don't tell me you're having second thoughts."

"I...I'm not sure," Anne admitted.

"Well, let me know before I make a deal."

While Anne loved the angel, ten thousand dollars or more for one of her pieces would go a long way toward establishing her credibility in the art world.

"I've been offered twenty-five thousand for it," Marta announced.

Anne felt faint. "How much?"

"You heard me right."

"I—I can't believe it! You've got to be making this up."

"No, and the bid is climbing."

"Marta, I have no idea what to say."

"Just let me know when your flight's coming in and I'll be there to pick you up, check in hand. We *do* want to sell this painting, don't we?"

Because she knew it was the right thing, Anne

said, "Yes, we do." Burton would probably never hear about her success, but that didn't matter. Anne Fletcher was an artist and an unusual one at that. She could support herself with what she made on her paintings.

CHAPTER NINETEEN

ROY CAUGHT HIMSELF whistling as he dressed for work Monday morning. He took a long look at himself in the mirror and saw something he hadn't seen in years. *Happiness.* It had sneaked up on him and could only be attributed to his relationship with Julie. He liked the way she made him feel, the way she challenged him and made him laugh. He liked her warmth and honesty. He'd discovered that he wanted to be with her more and more—all the time, in fact. And this had happened in only a few weeks. He often found himself impatient when they were apart, eager to be with her again. Suddenly he wanted—no, needed—to hear the sound of her voice.

Without thinking he picked up the phone.

Julie answered on the second ring.

"What are you doing?" he asked, keeping his voice low.

"Roy, it's six o'clock in the morning. I'm getting ready for school. What do you suppose I'm doing?"

"I was hoping you were thinking of me." He straddled a kitchen chair, grabbing his coffee mug.

The best Colombian coffee and conversation with Julie—not a bad way to start his day.

"I *was* thinking of you," she admitted reluctantly.

"Will you have dinner with me tonight?"

"I've got a game."

"After the game?"

"I'd love to."

His heart soared at the excitement he heard in her voice. Then again, it could be an echo of his own joy. He shook his head. This was crazy. He knew better than to let himself be swayed by feelings, especially feelings for a woman. Hadn't he learned that by now? Yet here he was, falling head over heels for Julie and he was doing it with his eyes wide open. A rational voice in his mind urged him to resist before he made another costly mistake. But a louder and more persistent voice promised him Julie was different....

"Where do you want to go?" he asked.

"Do we have to go anywhere?" she asked. "Dad's meeting some friends tonight. I can cook."

"After teaching all day and coaching a soccer game, you won't feel like cooking. Let me take you out."

"Nonsense. I'll start a stew in the Crock-Pot and it'll be ready when I get home from school."

Roy hadn't had regular home-cooked meals since he was a teenager. His mother, no matter how busy she was, had insisted on dinners together as a family. More often than not, his father had business to attend to, but Roy had always eaten with his mother, at least until he left for college in Seattle.

"Unless you don't want stew? I just thought it was a great wintertime meal and—"

"Your stew's wonderful," he assured her. She could serve dill pickles and he wouldn't have cared. All Roy wanted was to spend time with Julie. He had no idea where this was going and for the moment contented himself with the thrill of the ride.

They agreed to meet at her house at seven. Roy found himself watching the clock all day. The morning seemed to crawl, and his mind wasn't on his various meetings or the decisions he had to make. Even Ms. Johnson commented.

Roy brushed away her concern. He didn't admit it was Julie Wilcoff who occupied his thoughts, but he suspected Ms. Johnson had guessed as much.

That evening, at one minute to seven, Roy stood on Julie's front porch, clutching a bottle of excellent wine, and rang the doorbell. She answered almost immediately, her hair still wet from the shower. She'd combed it away from her face, and he noticed again how lovely she was, even without makeup. Her skin was smooth and healthy, her eyes bright, and her lips, with only the slightest color, looked as if they ached to be kissed. He knew *he* ached to kiss her. She wore slacks and a green sweater, and just seeing her turned his blood to steam. This was what he'd been looking forward to all day, what he'd wanted from the moment he'd climbed out of bed that morning.

"You're right on time," she said, reaching for his free hand. With a slight tug she brought him into the house.

Roy saw that he'd been standing on the porch like a schoolboy, simply staring at her. He knew he should wait before he kissed her, but he couldn't help himself. He set the wine on a hallway table crowded with gloves and unopened mail, and without even removing his coat, he brought her into his arms.

Julie went willingly to him and when their lips met, it was the first time that day he'd felt completely relaxed. She melted against him and he felt the soft fullness of her breasts against his chest. His hands craved their weight; he wanted to taste her nipples and watch them harden at his exploration. His head swam. The sensation their kisses evoked in him nearly sent him over the edge.

After several minutes, Julie pulled her mouth from his. "I...I've got bread under the broiler."

Only then did Roy smell the burning bread. He released her and, because his knees felt weak, walked into the living room and sat down. Shrugging off his coat, he struggled to regain his equilibrium. A moment later, he carried his overcoat to the hall closet and collected the wine, which he placed on the coffee table.

Julie returned just as he sat down again. "Thankfully I picked up two loaves of bread,'' she said. Offering him a shy smile, she started to walk past him to the chair opposite his.

Roy grabbed her hand, weaving his fingers through hers. ''I want to talk.''

''All right.'' Her dark eyes were solemn.

He drew her into his lap and resumed the kissing they'd begun in the hallway. Cradling her, he slipped his hand beneath her sweater and groaned as he encountered her breasts. His kisses turned greedy and urgent and—

A loud *ding* startled him and he broke off the kiss.

''That's the oven timer,'' Julie explained, and gazed at him, her eyes warm. ''Don't let it interrupt you.'' She frowned playfully. ''On the other hand, I don't want to burn my last loaf of bread.'' She slid off his lap and hurried to the kitchen. ''Hold that kiss—I mean thought,'' she called over her shoulder.

Roy grinned when she came back and returned to her position on his lap. ''I was serious about wanting to talk,'' he said after a quick kiss.

''I can see that,'' she teased.

''The problem is, you're too damn tempting.''

She rolled her eyes, but the smile didn't leave her lips. ''What do you want to talk about?''

''I can't think when we're this close.''

''Would you like me to move?''

''No...yes.'' It wasn't what he wanted, but it was necessary.

"All right." She slid off his lap a second time and sat on the sofa across from him.

"How long do you intend to live with your father?" he asked, leaning forward.

The question appeared to surprise her, and her eyes widened. "I...I was thinking of renting an apartment after the first of the year."

"Don't," he said.

Her eyes narrowed. "Why not? Dad needs to make his own life now and—"

"Move in with me." He hadn't broached the subject with much finesse, but he saw no reason to wait.

Julie didn't answer right away and her silence unnerved him.

"I take it you're not looking for a roommate to share expenses," she said in what was presumably an effort at humor.

"We both know what I'm asking."

"Yes...well." She took a breath and then slowly exhaled. "We...only met a few weeks ago."

"We know how we feel—what we want."

She lowered her gaze rather than confess the truth.

"Julie," he said, "we're adults."

Slowly she raised her eyes to meet his, and he read her indecision. Hoping to persuade her, he stood up and crossed to the sofa, sitting close beside her. Clasping Julie's hands, he brushed his mouth over hers. "We'd be good together," he whispered.

"I think so, too."

"Then why the hesitation?"

She cast down her gaze and shook her head.

"Come on," he urged. "Tell me."

"I'd hate to disappoint my father—I don't know how he'd feel about this."

Roy wanted to remind her that she was thirty years old and fully capable of making decisions without consulting her father. In any event, based on what he knew of Dean Wilcoff, the man wouldn't stand in their way.

"I'm afraid he'd do something rash," Julie explained.

"Like what?" Roy couldn't imagine him doing any such thing. Dean was a sensible man. He wouldn't intrude on his daughter's life. He'd accept whatever Julie wanted and keep his mouth shut—as he should.

"He wouldn't approve."

"So?"

"So," she continued, "I suspect he'd quit his job."

"That decision is his, don't you think?"

"Yes," she agreed after a lengthy pause. "But he needs this job and for more than the money. It's been wonderful for him, Roy. I'm so grateful you gave Dad a chance to feel productive again. It's been exactly what he needed."

"Leave your father to me," he told her. Roy would square the situation with Dean and make sure he had no objections. They could talk it out, man to man.

Still Julie hesitated.

"You don't need to decide right this minute. Take a few days, think it over. I'm not going to withdraw the offer."

A tremulous smile lifted the corners of her mouth. Roy was disappointed by her lack of excitement, although he wouldn't admit it. He'd hoped Julie would show as much enthusiasm for his idea as he felt himself.

Then it hit him. Naturally she was hesitant. She wanted it all, especially that ring on her finger, before she moved in with him.

"You want me to marry you first, don't you?"

"That's the way it's generally done," she said. "So...yes, I guess I do."

He appreciated her honesty and felt he couldn't be any less honest with her. "Sorry, Julie, it isn't going to happen. I'm not interested in marriage."

She took the news easily enough.

"All right," she said, her voice just a bit unsteady. "But what exactly are you offering me?"

Roy shrugged. "I'm offering you a place in my life and in my home. I'll be generous and attentive." He couldn't think of anything else she'd want. Although he hadn't spelled it out, he intended to give her all the things women often craved. She could buy whatever she wanted: jewels, clothes, cars. He didn't care.

''I don't doubt that you'd be good to me.''

''Then what's the problem?''

''For how long?''

His patience was slipping. ''You want guarantees?''

''Six weeks? Three months? A year?''

''How the hell am I supposed to know? For however long the two of us last.'' That should satisfy her. The way he felt just then, it could be a very long time, but she was right—maybe it wouldn't. Who could tell?

''You've done contracts with other businesses, right?''

Roy had the feeling she was thinking out loud. ''Yes—''

''You were ready to make a commitment to them, right?''

''Yes—''

''But you aren't willing to make a commitment to me.''

Ah, he was beginning to understand. ''I can break a contract for a price. Is that what you're talking about?''

''Are you suggesting payment?''

He should have wised up by now, but she'd had him fooled. Still, he didn't care. He was a man accustomed to paying for what he wanted. At the moment that was Julie, and he wanted her badly.

''Fine,'' he said. ''We can draw up a financial agreement.''

She shook her head and pulled her hands free of his. "That wasn't what I meant. I don't think you realize how insulting that suggestion is, Roy."

"Insulting? I thought it was what you wanted. Okay," he said, doing his best to figure her out. "Just tell me what it would take—other than marrying you—to get you to move in with me." He couldn't make it any plainer than that. Aimee had moved in without a moment's hesitation. He couldn't understand why Julie needed all this discussion.

"I don't know... I want to think this through." As if in a daze, she stood and walked slowly back to the kitchen.

Roy followed her. This night wasn't going the way he'd anticipated. He'd never been much good with relationships, and his experience with Aimee hadn't helped.

"What about love?" she asked, suddenly turning around.

Roy had come to detest the word. He didn't know what it was anymore. "Julie, you're searching for an excuse, and I'm not going to give it to you. You're looking for ways to talk yourself out of something we both want. This would be an agreement between two mature people who are strongly attracted to each other. Nothing more and nothing less."

"What about your mother?"

"What about her? She'd be thrilled. She's been

saying for a long time that I work too hard, and she's right. Knowing her, she'll kiss you on both cheeks and thank you.''

Julie didn't seem to believe him.

''If it's any consolation, you should know I've only had one other woman live with me.'' Aimee. And whatever happened with Julie, it couldn't possibly end as badly as *that* relationship.

Taking two bowls and two wineglasses from the cupboard, Julie set them on the counter. ''I want to think this through,'' she said again. She gave him a weak smile. ''Like you said, this offer is good for more than twenty-four hours.''

''Take all the time you need.'' But he wanted her in his home and in his bed. The sooner the better.

CHAPTER TWENTY

"I DON'T KNOW about anyone else," Goodness said, still in a huff, pacing inside Roy's office. "But I'm outraged." She fluttered her wings just so her friends would know she wasn't kidding.

Papers slid off Roy's desk and he looked up, clearly puzzled by the sudden draft.

"Roy's a man," Mercy chided her, far too willing to overlook his weaknesses. "What do you expect?"

"And I'm an angel," Goodness said right back. "What do *you* expect?"

"These are human matters," Shirley insisted, lurking around the back of Roy's chair. "We can't get involved."

"Julie knows better. Mark my words—she'll refuse to do it."

Mercy sighed expressively and sat on the corner of Roy's fancy desk, protecting his files from further disruption. "I wouldn't be so sure if I were you. She's tempted."

"Then we'll untempt her."

Shirley shook her head. "That's not our department. They send in the Warrior Angels to deal with temptations."

True, but Goodness had intense feelings when it came to the humans involved in her prayer requests. Shirley, Goodness and Mercy had worked hard to bring these two together. She no longer felt any uncertainty about their choice; Julie was the woman Anne had prayed for. After all their efforts, the least Roy could do was marry her! Time was running out. They had to think of something quickly if he was going to propose by Christmas Eve. After that, they were off the case. Oh, dear, this could turn into a real disaster and of course Gabriel would blame the three of them.

"We've got to make Julie see sense," Goodness said. If Mercy was right, then Julie might indeed give in to the temptation. The prayer request was ambiguous; Anne hadn't stated that Roy needed to marry this woman, although it was implied.

"He hasn't heard from her in two days." Mercy flipped the pages of Roy's desktop calendar.

"Don't do that," Goodness cried, slapping Mercy's hand. "He might see you."

Mercy tilted her head and stared at Roy Fletcher. "He's deep in thought."

"He's wondering how long it'll take to hear from Julie," Shirley suggested. "He's growing impatient."

Goodness had noticed that, but she also knew he'd done nothing to get in touch with Julie. She suspected this was a ploy on his part—his way of telling Julie that if she chose to reject his offer, she wouldn't be hearing from him again. That was just plain wrong! Goodness intended to do everything within her power to make sure Roy's head was filled with thoughts of Julie every minute of every day. The man would be sorry he'd messed with her plans to answer his mother's prayer.

"You know how cold he can be," Shirley commented, studying Roy intently. She shivered and wrapped her arms around herself.

"That's all an act," Goodness told them. "He loves his mother and Julie, only he's too stubborn to admit it."

"I say we get in there and do something," Mercy proclaimed.

"Like what?" Goodness was almost afraid to ask.

"What we always do." Mercy folded her hands prayerfully and fluttered her long, curly eyelashes.

"Heaven help us," Goodness muttered.

"No, you've got it all wrong," Mercy said. "*We're* the ones helping Heaven. Gabriel needs us. Otherwise, we'd be long gone by now. I for one feel that drastic times call for drastic measures."

"Drastic measures," Goodness repeated. "What—"

"Stand back everyone." Mercy threw open her wings.

"What's she going to do?" Goodness asked Shirley. "Toss a fish at him?"

Shirley giggled.

Just when Mercy was getting ready to make her

move, Ms. Johnson entered Roy's office. The three angels glided out of the way as his assistant handed him a sheaf of papers that required his signature.

"Ms. Johnson," he said as the woman was about to leave, "would you mind if I asked you a couple of questions?"

"Are they personal questions?" she asked hesitantly.

"Not exactly personal. Did you tell me you have a daughter in her twenties?"

"I do. Janice. She recently turned twenty-three. What makes you ask?"

"I was just wondering if—" He was interrupted by someone knocking on the partially opened door.

Shirley gasped.

"Who's that?" Goodness wanted to know.

"I think it might be Aimee," Mercy told her in a hushed whisper.

Indeed it was. The woman who'd dumped Roy for his father. She stepped into the office wearing a full-length mink coat and high-heel shoes. She was sleek, petite and very blond. They didn't call it *platinum* blond for nothing, Goodness thought spitefully.

"What's *she* doing here?" No one answered, and Goodness suspected her friends were as surprised as Roy obviously was.

He slowly stood. "That will be all, Ms. Johnson."

"Yes, sir." His assistant hurried out of the room.

"Hello, Roy." Aimee smiled seductively and walked up to his desk. "It's good to see you."

"How did you get into the building?"

"Oh, I have my ways."

Roy snickered. "I'll just bet you do." He made a mental note to talk to Dean Wilcoff about this.

"I think it's time we talked, don't you?" Without waiting for an invitation, she sat down and crossed her shapely legs.

Roy remained standing. "Actually, I think it's time you left."

Aimee sighed deeply. "There's no need to be nasty."

"I mean it, Aimee."

She shook her head, her long, blond hair swinging softly from side to side. "Roy, this is ridiculous! You refuse to have anything to do with your father—"

"I have nothing to say to him *or* to you."

"That's sad, because we both want to reconcile with you."

His gaze narrowed. "I don't think I can bring myself to call you Mother."

She laughed, shrugging off his sarcasm. "I don't think you should. Tell me, how are you?"

"Fine. Now leave."

"I've come all this way, and I'm not going until you talk to me."

Roy lowered himself stiffly into his chair. "What do you want?"

Aimee's expression became petulant. "I always hated it when you used that tone of voice with me." As if she suddenly felt hot, she unfastened the buttons of her coat and slipped her arms free.

Roy stared at the mink and at the silk suit beneath, set off by a stunning emerald brooch. "I see Daddy's buying you lots of gifts."

Aimee shrugged one elegant shoulder. "You might not believe this, but I happen to love your father."

Roy raised his eyes to the ceiling. "Yeah, and I'll bet you love his bank balance even more." He'd understood long ago that Aimee had set her sights on his father from the beginning of their so-called relationship. He'd been used, and it wasn't going to happen again.

Her lips thinned. "You can insult me all you want, but I will not take offense. I came because I want to build a bridge between you and your father."

Roy laughed outright. "The woman who blew up the bridge now wants to build one? I find that interesting."

"It's true, Roy. It's been five years. Your father and I have a very good life, but he misses you." She pouted ever so slightly.

"Why am I having trouble believing that?"

"It's true," Aimee said a second time, even more insistently. "Talk to your father, okay? It's what he wants. Me, too. I'd like us all to be friends."

"I'd like world peace myself."

"Burton *is* your father."

"He made his choice and I've made mine."

Aimee reached for her purse and removed a gold cigarette case. "Do you mind if I smoke?"

"I thought you quit."

"I am quitting."

"You were quitting five years ago."

She tapped the cigarette against the case and then inserted it between her lips. "It isn't easy, you know."

"This is a nonsmoking building."

"Whatever," she muttered, returning the cigarette to the case, which she thrust back in her purse.

"Just finish saying what you came here to say and then get out."

She looked genuinely hurt. "Burton wants to see you."

Roy didn't consider the request. "What for?" he asked scornfully.

"You're his son. He loves you."

Roy frowned. "He has a unique way of showing his love. Let me see… I love my son. I wonder how I can best show him that love? I know! I'll divorce my wife, destroy my family and steal his fiancée. That should do the trick. Well, guess what, it didn't work."

"Roy, don't you understand that what happened between me and your father just *happened?* Neither of us asked to fall in love with the other."

Roy's hand shot up. "Spare me. I don't buy that for a second. You no more love my father than you loved me. When I think of what a fool I was, I get sick to my stomach. It was never me you wanted. I see that now. You were always interested in my father and you used me to get to him."

Aimee flew to her feet. "That's where you're wrong. I *do* love Burton and he loves me. I love him enough to swallow my pride and approach you. Just talk to him, that's all I ask."

"Sorry, but I'm not interested."

"I'd hoped your mother—"

"Leave my mother out of this!"

"I sent her a Christmas card," Aimee said. "I thought the best way to reach you was through her."

Roy stood up and leaned against his desk. "You sent my mother a Christmas card? I can't believe you'd do such a thing. How was she supposed to take that?"

"I didn't write anything in it. I just wanted her to know I don't bear her any ill will."

Roy stared at Aimee, completely stupefied. "Did it ever occur to you that she might be the one who bears ill will?"

Aimee bit her pouting lower lip. Collagen injections? he wondered indifferently. "Not really."

"Thank God you never wanted to be *her* friend. I'd hate to think what you might have done if you'd actually liked her."

Aimee gave a little cry of dismay. ‘‘I didn’t do anything to her!’’

Despite his effort not to reveal his emotions, Roy felt himself clenching his jaw. ‘‘You stole her husband.’’

‘‘I didn’t,’’ Aimee insisted. ‘‘Burton hadn’t been happy in years.’’

Roy ignored that. ‘‘Then my father cheats my mother in the divorce settlement. He took what should’ve been hers by hiding the money in offshore accounts.’’

‘‘Burton would never do that,’’ Aimee said, shaking her head. The shimmering pale-blond hair swung gently as she did. Roy supposed she was well aware of the effect.

‘‘Stay married to him,’’ he advised. ‘‘Now you know what he’ll do if a younger, sexier replacement comes along.’’

‘‘Burton and I are deeply in love,’’ Aimee said. ‘‘Do you think it was easy coming here today? Well, it wasn’t. I thought—I hoped you’d at least listen to me, but I can see I was wrong.’’

‘‘You can tell my father one thing,’’ Roy said angrily. ‘‘Tell him to—’’

‘‘I DON’T WANT to listen,’’ Shirley cried, and covered both her ears.

‘‘Me, neither.’’ Goodness followed suit. She hummed a special hymn to blot out the terse, angry words. When she felt it was safe, she lifted her hands from her ears.

Mercy's eyes were wide. "That boy has quite the vocabulary."

"You listened?"

"Sure, why not? Aimee had it coming. That woman has some nerve, arriving like that out of the blue."

Shirley walked over to the door and peered out. "She's gone now."

"Good riddance."

"What a mess," Goodness said with a sigh. "I think she must genuinely love Roy's father, otherwise she'd never have shown up at the office."

"She lacks discretion," Shirley said sadly. "How could she possibly think that mailing Anne a Christmas card would help her cause?"

"She's feeling guilty."

"As well she should."

"We weren't sent here to deal with Aimee," Goodness reminded her friends. "That woman is going to require an entire legion of angels. Our concern is helping Roy."

"Oh, brother!" Mercy threw herself against the wall. "You won't believe this."

"What?" Shirley tried to peek but Mercy stopped her. "Oh, look at Roy."

Goodness studied him. Roy was in an agitated state, pacing back and forth across the room. Although she was unable to read his thoughts, one glance told her that those thoughts were dark and angry.

Mercy pointed toward the other room. "You'll never guess who just arrived."

"Not Anne," Shirley cried.

"No, worse," Mercy said, covering her eyes. "It's Julie."

CHAPTER TWENTY-ONE

JULIE STEPPED OFF the elevator and strolled toward Ms. Johnson, the guardian of Roy's office. For two days, she'd wrestled with the question of what she should do. She dreaded giving him her answer, but now that she was here, she was more convinced than ever that she'd made the right decision.

Her natural inclination was to accept Roy's invitation and move in with him. He was correct about one thing: it was what they both wanted. Deep down, she clung to the hope that one day he'd love her. She suspected he already did, or had begun to, anyway, but refused to acknowledge his feelings. Moving in with him had been easy to rationalize. In the end, however, after a lengthy talk with her sister, Julie accepted that she wanted more out of their relationship. The hard part would be convincing Roy that they both needed more time.

"Ms. Wilcoff." His assistant looked up, startled. "Did I know you were coming?"

"No, no, I stopped here on my way home from school. Is Roy busy?"

The woman, who was rarely flustered, seemed so now. "Let me check." Rather than use the intercom, she scurried away from her desk and disappeared behind Roy's office door.

When Jason, the downstairs security guard, had let Julie into the building without so much as a raised eyebrow, she should've realized there was a problem. The guard wore a funny look, as if he knew something she didn't. Julie had wanted to ask him, but decided against it. Now Ms. Johnson was behaving in a peculiar manner, too.

A moment later, she reappeared. "He asked me to show you right in, but..."

"But?" Julie prompted when the woman hesitated. "Is Roy having a bad day?"

The older woman nodded. "You could say that. On second thought, seeing you might be exactly what he needs."

Now that Julie had arrived at her decision, she felt an urgency to get this conversation over with as quickly as possible. Delaying it might give her just enough time to change her mind.

Roy was sitting at his desk when she entered his office. He looked up and smiled, but she noticed that the warmth she'd grown to expect was missing.

"Should I come back later?" she asked uncertainly.

"No." He motioned for her to take a seat.

"I probably should've phoned first."

"Probably," he agreed. He relaxed in his chair and folded his hands over his stomach. And waited.

"I thought I should let you know what I've decided."

He nodded, his expression unchanged.

The tightness in Julie's throat increased. She leaned forward just a little and tucked her hands beneath her thighs, something she did when she was nervous. "I guess there's only one way to say this..."

"You decided against accepting my invitation," he finished for her.

"Yes."

"Any particular reason?"

"Several, but I do want you to know how tempted I was."

"That's neither here nor there, is it?"

"Well, no—"

"Unless, of course, you're figuring I'll up the ante."

Anger flared instantly, but Julie mentally counted to ten before responding. "No, Roy, I'm not figuring you'll up the ante." She stood. "I think it'd be best if we talked about this another time."

"Now is as good as any," he insisted.

She leaned closer to his desk, desperately searching his face for the reason he'd changed. "What's wrong with you?"

"Me?" he demanded.

"You're looking at me like...like I've sprouted horns or something."

He laughed, but even his laughter sounded sarcastic. "All right, I'll play your little game. What would it take to get you into my condo? A monthly allowance? Jewelry? Just tell me and I'll arrange it."

"Don't insult me!"

"Is a thousand a week enough? You can quit teaching, live a life of luxury."

"I happen to like my job."

He snorted. "You don't have to give up teaching. Why should I care as long as you're there when I want you?"

Julie was beginning to feel sick. "I think I'd better leave."

"Don't go," he said, although he didn't offer her a reason to stay.

"What happened?" she asked, and made a sweeping gesture with her right arm. "Something must have happened."

"You mean other than an unexpected visit from my *stepmother?*" He dragged out the last word, as if even saying it was repugnant.

"Oh." He was talking about Aimee—which explained a great deal. "So you're back to that."

He arched one brow. "That?"

"All women are users and manipulators and not to be trusted, and therefore you ridicule every female you meet." She'd had enough. When Roy was in this frame of mind, there was no reasoning with him, as she knew from experience. She turned to leave.

Roy bolted out of his chair. "Where are you going?"

She ignored the question. "I'm leaving. Perhaps we can talk when you're feeling less…angry."

"No, I want this settled today."

"Then it's settled. You have my answer." She started toward the door.

"I don't accept that."

Julie faced him and slowly shook her head. "You know what? There are some things in this life you can't buy, and I'm one of them."

He scoffed. "You'll change your mind."

Rather than argue with him, she simply walked away. She was so furious her head felt about to explode. Mingled with the anger was a profound hurt. Roy didn't respect her, let alone love her. He viewed her as an object he could control—and then discard when he'd finished.

"Julie?" Ms. Johnson stood as Julie walked by.

Numb now, she only half heard the other woman. All Julie wanted was to escape. She moved rapidly toward the elevator, hitting the down button.

"I shouldn't have let you see him," Ms. Johnson said anxiously. "He hasn't had a good afternoon."

"Don't make excuses for him," Julie told her, stepping into the elevator. As soon as the doors closed, she slumped against the wall. Everything had become clear. She knew that some people were unable to move past the pain inflicted by others. They carried it with them for the rest of their lives, and everyone they met, everything they accomplished, was blighted by that pain. Roy, sadly, was one of those people.

When the elevator reached the lobby, Julie straightened, eager to get away from Fletcher Industries—and Fletcher. When the doors slid open, Jason stood directly in front of her, legs braced apart, hands on his hips.

"Mr. Fletcher would like to see you," he announced.

"Tell him another time would be better," Julie said, attempting to move past him.

"He insisted. I'm sorry, Ms. Wilcoff, but I have my orders."

"Which are what? Shoot me on sight if I refuse to talk to your boss? This is illegal confinement, in case you weren't aware of it."

A smile cracked Jason's tight lips. "Just talk to him, all right?"

"I'm supposed to take the elevator up to his office?"

Jason nodded.

"I won't do that."

Jason's eyes pleaded with her. "As a personal favor to me, would you just do it?"

"Sorry, no."

"Ms. Wilcoff, he called down here himself and asked me to keep you in the building."

Julie laughed despite herself. "That's quite a contrast to his earlier commands, isn't it?"

"Can't help that." He shrugged. "I will say this—you've certainly made my job interesting."

Julie gave an exasperated sigh. Talking to Roy, especially now, wasn't going to solve anything. "I'm sorry, I can't." When it looked as if Jason was about to detain her, Julie leaped agilely to the right and then just as quickly to the left. To her astonishment, without the least bit of effort, she sprinted past the guard.

Jason appeared stunned. "How'd you do that?" he asked, chasing after her.

She was at the door, pushing it open, when he reached her. He stretched out his arms, lunged forward—and froze in place. "I can't move," he cried. "Something's holding me back."

"Good try, Jason," she said as she walked outside, taking a moment to admire Anne's angel windows. Too bad Roy didn't understand the spirit of Christmas—or the nature of faith and love—the way his mother did.

"I'm not joking!"

The door closed behind her as she hurried toward the visitor parking lot. She glanced over her shoulder once to find Jason still in that peculiar position, one leg stretched out as if stepping forward to grab her. When he noticed her watching him, he called out for help. Smiling, Julie simply shook her head. He certainly had an inventive approach to getting her sympathy.

After she drove away from Fletcher Industries,

Julie headed toward the school. It was almost dark now, but she needed to vent her frustration, so she changed into running gear and started toward the track. After doing a couple of quick laps, she left the field and took one of her usual routes in a friendly neighborhood near the school. Generally she avoided running in the dark, but her gear had reflective tape so she could be seen by oncoming traffic.

Her feet hit the pavement in a rhythm that matched the pounding of her heart. Her thoughts, however, flew at a far greater speed. Anger was soon replaced by sadness. Sadness became regret…and resignation. When she reached the five-mile marker, she became aware of a car driving behind her.

It could only be Roy.

He eased his car alongside her and slid down the passenger window. "You have a hard time following directions, don't you?"

"Not at all." She slowed to a clipped walk, her arms swinging. "Why would you say that?"

"What did you do to Jason?"

"I didn't do a thing to him."

Roy eased his sedan to a stop, parked it by the curb and then jumped out. Jogging around the front of the vehicle, he joined her. "That's not what he told me."

"Believe what you want." She tried to hide how hard she was breathing—and how pleased she was to see him. Because, in spite of everything, she was. But that wasn't going to change the situation.

"Come on, Julie, be reasonable. If you want an apology, you've got one. I was rude and arrogant." He paced his walk to hers.

"Yes, you were."

"Thank you for being so gracious," he muttered.

"I don't think we've got anything left to discuss. You have my answer."

"I want to change your mind."

"It wouldn't work," she said, and she meant it. She stopped walking, and at the risk of letting down her guard, raised her hand to his cheek. "In the beginning, living together would've been wonderful—"

"It still can be."

"But it wouldn't last."

"Nothing lasts forever, and we'd be foolish to think otherwise."

"My parents' love for each other did."

"Mine didn't."

Julie shook her head. "I'm sorry for you, sorry for them, but I can't let what happened between your mother and father taint *my* life. I'm falling in love with you, Roy, and I want it all."

With an angry sigh of frustration, he threw back his head to stare at the dark sky. "Julie, come on! I'm willing to give you whatever you want."

"But that's just the point—you aren't."

He placed his hand over hers and raised it to his

lips, kissing the tender skin of her palm. "We could have something good. Who cares if it doesn't last a lifetime?"

"I care, Roy. I'm sorry, I really am. It would be so easy to let you persuade me, but in the end I'd have nothing left except a broken heart." He couldn't possibly know how much she already loved him.

Roy released her hand. "You're like all the rest, aren't you? You want to control me, get your hands on my success and make it your own. Naturally, your term for this is *love.* I'm supposed to marry you and promise to spend the rest of my life with you? Well, you can forget that."

"Yup, the old marriage trap. It's worked for thousands of years, but it's not good enough for you. Silly me for refusing to settle for anything less than love and commitment." She gestured wildly with one hand.

"I can't do it, Julie."

"I know."

"Then there's nothing more to say."

"Obviously not." Her throat constricted with sadness.

Neither moved. Neither wanted to be the first to turn away, Julie suspected, or to acknowledge that this relationship was over almost before it had begun.

Finally she was the one who turned and, with tears burning her eyes, ran in the opposite direction.

CHAPTER TWENTY-TWO

SATURDAY AFTERNOON, Christmas music played softly in the background as Anne pulled her suitcase from the closet and laid it on her bed. She sang along with her favorite carols as she started to take sweaters from her dresser drawers. Since Marta had sent her the airline ticket, she'd had two other phone conversations with her. Things seemed to be looking up. Jack had made numerous attempts to speak to her and she'd agreed to meet with him—after she got the report from the private investigator. Naturally she didn't tell him that part; Jack had no idea his wife was having him followed. Their conversation would depend on what the investigator told Marta. Still, Jack's willingness—indeed frantic desire—to get his wife back, boded well, Anne thought. She was grateful Marta could benefit from her experience.

Marta hadn't given Anne any new details regarding the sale of her angel portrait. However, from everything her friend had told her, the news was good. The painting would definitely sell, and for a good price, too.

A noise in the living room startled Anne, and she

paused to listen again. Someone was in her home. ‘‘Who’s there?’’ she called out, a little nervous. She tried to remember where she’d left her portable phone.

‘‘Mother?’’

‘‘Roy?’’ She hurried out of the bedroom. ‘‘What are you doing here?’’ Her son’s appearance shocked her. He hadn’t shaved in a day or two and looked as if he’d slept in his clothes.

‘‘Frankly, I don’t know,’’ he said, not meeting her eyes. ‘‘I started driving and then all of a sudden I was on a ferry, headed to your place. I guess I just need to talk.’’

‘‘My goodness, what’s happened?’’ she asked, resisting the urge to take him in her arms.

‘‘I wasn’t sure if you’d already left for New York or not.’’

‘‘I fly out in the morning. Now, sit down and tell me what’s wrong.’’ For once he didn’t argue. She directed him into her kitchen, sat him down at the small table and immediately started cooking. At times like this, food could be a wonderful comfort. She put on a pot of coffee, then took out a pan and set it on the stove, followed by two eggs from the refrigerator. When she noticed that she was paying more attention to creating the perfect omelet than to her son, she stopped. She pulled out a chair and sat across from Roy.

‘‘What is it?’’ she asked gently.

‘‘I asked Julie to move in with me,’’ he mumbled.

Anne sighed heavily. That wasn't what she wanted for her son; in fact, she saw such an action as a mistake for both of them, but young people always thought they knew best.

"You don't approve. Julie knew her father wouldn't, either, not that it matters, anyway."

"She turned you down?"

"Lock, stock and barrel. I guess I should be grateful."

He certainly didn't *look* grateful. If anything, Roy seemed distraught. Immediate questions came to mind, but Anne avoided asking, knowing Roy would explain everything in his own time. "I'm sorry, son."

"So am I. Julie insists on what she calls love and, of course, marriage." He spit out the words as if they tasted foul.

"You've had setbacks before," Anne said, hardly able to credit this kind of reaction to a simple rejection. Privately Anne was cheering Julie for having the courage to hold out for what she wanted. It must have been very difficult to turn him down. When Roy went after something, he usually did it with a determination that was difficult to ignore.

"This is more than a setback."

"How do you mean?"

Roy rubbed a hand tiredly down his face and shook his head. "I was foolish enough to believe she was different."

"Julie *is* special. I know you think every woman's like Aimee, but you're wrong."

''No, Mother, in Julie's case I'm right.''

''Julie isn't anything like Aimee,'' she said adamantly.

''She just proved to me she is.''

''What do you mean?'' He'd have to show her the evidence before Anne would believe him. Although she didn't know Julie well, Anne had sensed genuine goodness in her. She felt, too, that Julie had attained the spiritual and emotional insights that only someone who'd suffered could fully understand.

Roy reached inside his jacket and pulled out a wad of folded papers. ''Read this.''

Anne took the papers, opening them on the table. She put on her reading glasses and quickly scanned the contents. As far as she could see, it was a bunch of legal mumbo jumbo. ''It's some sort of settlement offer,'' she said. ''Oh, here's Julie's name.''

''I know what it is,'' Roy barked, then cast her an apologetic glance. ''Remember when I ran into her?''

''Yes, of course, your car collided with her bike. It's a miracle she wasn't hurt.''

He gave an unpleasant laugh. ''Correction, Mother. She was hurt twenty-five-thousand dollars' worth.''

Anne snatched up the papers and skimmed them again. ''What are you talking about?''

''She signed the settlement offer. A check's already been issued to her in the amount stated.''

Anne knew that wasn't possible. Yet there was Julie's signature, plain as day.

Roy focused his gaze on the kitchen wall. "I pressured her at first, believing it was best to deal with the incident quickly rather than have her come back and bite me later. She repeatedly refused, and after a while I started to trust her.

"I finally accepted that she wasn't a gold digger. She had me convinced that money didn't mean a thing to her—and now this."

"Roy, I don't think—"

"You're holding the evidence in your hand," he countered, his voice raised in anger.

Only he wasn't really angry, Anne realized; he was hurt and disillusioned and growing more so by the minute. Oh, this was dreadful. It was as if God had broken a promise. Anne had believed that Julie was the woman she'd been praying for all these years and now this…this betrayal.

"All along, Julie was holding out for more money." He rubbed his eyes as if he was exhausted. "I forgot about the settlement when we started dating." He expelled a shaky breath. "Then she declined to move in with me, and that was the end of our fine romance. Except that I remembered we hadn't settled her so-called accident and I contacted her again."

Anne didn't say anything, waiting for him to continue his story.

"She wouldn't talk to me about it."

Anne silently applauded; perhaps everything wasn't lost, after all.

"The thing is, Mother, I thought she was different, that I could trust her."

Anne reached across the table and patted his hand.

"Then she proved I can't."

"Roy, let's not be hasty here. Yes, it looks bad, but let's face it—if Julie was interested in your money, she would've moved in with you. Don't make the mistake of judging her too harshly."

"Harshly," he spat. "It isn't just about the money. I went over to her place to see her, to talk to her. I thought maybe we could find a way to compromise.... All I wanted was for the two of us to be together."

Anne bit her lower lip, afraid of what he'd say next.

"I told her if she didn't want to move in with me, I'd be willing to set her up in her own apartment."

After a moment, Anne managed to speak. "She wasn't interested in that, either, I take it."

"Not at all."

Anne smiled to herself. Perhaps, just perhaps, Julie was everything she'd hoped for. Surely God wouldn't be so cruel as to send another Aimee into Roy's life.

"I reminded her that I wasn't offering marriage, but she could have the next-best thing. I let it be known that this was my final offer. If she said no, I was walking out that door once and for all."

''She was willing to accept that?''

He hung his head. ''Apparently so. Then I brought up the settlement. I told her I wasn't upping the ante. If she was going to get anything out of me, she'd better sign.''

''You left the papers with her?''

''Yes,'' he said bitterly. ''I had my attorney contact her. This afternoon I got the signed papers by messenger, with the attorney's notice that the check had been mailed.''

Roy looked so disheartened Anne ached to take him in her arms the way she had when he was small. He'd come to her to seek solace, but that was of little comfort when there was nothing she could do or say to ease this pain. Julie hadn't turned out to be the woman Anne had hoped.

''She has her money, then?''

He nodded. ''It's what she always wanted. Twenty-five thou—no strings. I'll say one thing for her,'' he muttered cynically. ''She was good.''

Anne's shoulders sagged with disappointment. ''Live and learn,'' she said under her breath.

''She came in right after Aimee that afternoon,'' Roy said, speaking almost to himself.

Anne leaned closer, certain she'd misunderstood him. ''Aimee was five years ago.''

''No, Aimee was three days ago.''

Anne thought her heart had stopped beating. She needed a moment to calm herself before she asked, ''Aimee came to see you? Recently?''

Roy's gaze darted to hers. "I didn't mean to say anything—I shouldn't have. I apologize, Mom, for bringing up unpleasant memories."

"Tell me," Anne insisted.

Roy tilted back in his chair, staring at the ceiling. "She stopped by the office, unannounced and unwelcome."

"Whatever for?"

"Why does Aimee do anything?" Roy said with a deep edge of sarcasm. "She wanted something."

"What?"

Roy shook his head as if to say he still didn't really believe it. "She came with some ridiculous story about my father loving me and wanting to see me again."

"I know Burton's tried to contact you," Anne said.

"Who told you that?"

She didn't want to get his assistant in trouble, but Ms. Johnson had volunteered the information. "It wouldn't do you any harm to talk to him, you know."

"I don't have anything to say to the man," Roy said bluntly.

Anne felt herself go rigid. "It's been five years since you last talked to your father. I know you don't want to hear this, but I think it's time you two called a truce." As difficult as it was, she gave Aimee credit for supporting Burton's desire to make peace with his son.

"We don't have anything in common."

"He's your *father.*"

"He betrayed us both."

Anne didn't have a response to that. She wasn't in any position to defend Burton, and wouldn't. "At least Aimee tried to help."

Roy snickered. "Don't go painting her in any chivalrous light. She had her own agenda. She always has. I should've recognized it at the time, but fool that I am, I took her at face value."

"What do you mean?"

Roy looked away, as if he'd said more than he intended. "I called Dad."

"Oh, Roy, I'm so glad you did." Part of that was a lie, but for Roy's sake she was grateful. A son, no matter what his age, needed his father.

He shook his head. "The conversation didn't go well, but I did learn an important piece of information."

Anne waited for him to explain.

"Aimee wants something big and expensive for Christmas, and Dad told her if he was going to plunk down thousands of dollars, she could do something for him."

"I see."

"He got what *he* wanted," Roy murmured. "I phoned him, just like she knew I would."

Aimee's manipulativeness had left Roy deeply cynical toward women; Julie's actions, unfortunately, had only confirmed that cynicism.

"How is your father?" Anne asked despite herself.

"You honestly care?" Roy stared at her, his eyes skeptical. "The man betrayed you, cheated you, and now you're concerned about his well-being? Don't be, Mother. Dad is getting exactly what he deserves."

"And what's that?"

He laughed. "Aimee. She's spending money faster than he can earn it."

"I'm sorry to hear that."

He cast her a doubting look.

Anne grinned. "Okay, that's not entirely true. But I really don't harbor any ill will toward your father. I've gotten on with my life. After the divorce, I felt used up and old, but now..." She got to her feet, still talking, and poured them each a coffee. "Well, the thing is, I found a whole new part of myself. I believe that our world was created with a sense of order. For every loss, there's a gain. Sometimes we're so blinded by the loss that we don't see the gain, don't recognize the gift." She paused, handing him his cup. "There's a wonderful gift for you in Aimee's betrayal, and one day you'll discover it."

Roy gazed at her with puzzlement and what seemed to be renewed respect. "You're a better person than I'll ever be."

Anne hated to ask again, but she was curious about her ex-husband. "Is your father...well?"

"What you really mean is, does he have any regrets?" Roy supplied for her.

There was some truth in that. "I don't think your father would admit any regrets to you, would he?"

Roy agreed. "Not in so many words, but it was easy enough to read between the lines."

Anne waited. So often she'd speculated about Burton and his new life. "Other than financially, is everything as it should be?"

"I don't think so. My guess is that Dad's having trouble keeping up with Aimee, uh, physically. Now that he's in his sixties, his work pace is taking its toll. He didn't sound happy."

"How *did* he sound?"

"Tired, exasperated, overworked."

"I thought your father would've retired by now."

"He can't," Roy said, "not with the speed at which Aimee is spending his money, and that's only the half of it."

"What do you mean?"

Roy shrugged and it seemed for a moment that he wasn't going to tell her. "It also seems that Aimee's taken a liking to some of his clients—men who are seeking solace after their divorces."

Anne was shocked. "Your father actually told you that?"

"Not in so many words, but close." He shook his head in disgust. "She spouted all these platitudes about loving my father and building a bridge between us, and it was all lies." A muscle leaped in the side of his jaw. "She came with a purpose, which she advanced with her lies. She wanted something from me, just the same as Julie did."

Obviously, it was Julie who was on his mind. "No matter what papers Julie signed," Anne said, "I still don't think she's anything like Aimee."

"I've been fooled before, and I'm not going to let it happen again."

"I know." It broke her heart to admit that. "I wish I wasn't leaving you over Christmas."

He frowned, and then smiled. "Do you honestly think it bothers me? Christmas doesn't mean a thing to me."

"But, Roy, it should." Her heart ached for her only child. Nothing had worked out as she'd hoped. Her prayers, like so many before, had gone unanswered. Roy would be alone on Christmas Day.

CHAPTER TWENTY-THREE

THREE DAYS before Christmas, Julie knew this was destined to be the worst one of her life. She was already dealing with the loss of her mother and now, it seemed she'd lost Roy, too.

Even her twin sister's call hadn't raised her spirits. Julie ended the conversation and then wandered into the living room, where her father sat watching the evening news.

One look at her, and Dean grabbed the remote control and muted the volume. "That bad?"

"I feel just awful."

"Because of Fletcher?"

Slumping into the chair next to him, Julie nodded. "I don't know what happened. I went to see him on Wednesday afternoon, and it was as if he'd shut me out of his life." Julie still didn't understand it. He'd been so cold and defensive; nothing she said reached him. And their second meeting, a day later, was even worse.

"Is it the settlement money?"

She shrugged. She'd never intended to accept a dime of that settlement, but Roy had angered her so much she'd agreed to his terms out of pure frustration. He seemed to believe all women were greedy for money and power.

"I was tired of fighting with him," she said in a subdued voice.

"I know. Fletcher's gone far in the business world by the sheer power of his determination."

"Only in this instance, he's wrong."

"I know, Kitten."

Her last angry exchange with Roy lingered in her mind. Furious, she'd signed those stupid settlement papers. It was what he'd expected, what he'd demanded she do—and so she had. But oh, how she regretted it. She hated to end their relationship on such a negative note, but what choice did she have? Roy had cast her from his life as if she meant nothing.

"I don't know if he's capable of love," she murmured, hoping her father had some consolation to offer.

"Every human has the capacity to love," he said with such confidence that her heart surged with hope. "But a person's ability to love is only equal to his or her openness in receiving love."

Julie valued her father's wisdom. He was right; nothing she could say or do at this point had the potential to reach Roy. He had certain beliefs about her and about all women, and he'd made certain assumptions as a result.

"I'd like one last opportunity to talk to him," she said. Not because she expected to change his mind.

That seemed doubtful. All she wanted was an opportunity to undo the damage they'd inflicted on each other.

Her father seemed to weigh her words. "Do you think seeing him again is wise?"

"I...don't know. Probably not," she said, but the need still burned within her. "I just feel so bad about the way we ended everything...."

"Fletcher has been out of the office for a few days, but I understand he's back now."

"It's almost Christmas and...in the spirit of the holidays I thought..."

"You thought he might listen?"

"At least long enough to understand my reasons."

"Do you want to do this for you or for Fletcher?" her father asked.

The question was a valid one. Julie mulled it over and then answered as honestly as she could. "I don't know. I guess it's for me. I don't feel right leaving things the way they are. I can't imagine he'll see me, but I have to try."

"Then write him a letter."

"A letter," Julie repeated. "I doubt he'd read it."

"Does that matter?" her father asked. "You'll have said what you feel is necessary. Then you can let him go."

"True," she admitted, the idea taking shape. The more she thought about it, the more she realized how much had been left unsaid. This was her opportunity to say what was in her heart.

"Whether Fletcher reads it or not is up to him. When feelings run this strong, sometimes letters are the best form of communication. There's less room for misunderstanding or argument."

Julie immediately felt relieved. Writing Roy, explaining her emotions and beliefs, was a solution she hadn't considered before. She might never learn whether or not he read her letter, but she'd have the satisfaction of knowing she'd done everything she could. If he responded, good; that would mean there was still a chance. If, as she expected, she never heard from him again, she could find peace in the knowledge that she'd tried.

"Oh, Dad, I don't think I appreciate you nearly enough."

Dean grinned and picked up the television remote. "Probably not," he said.

Composing the letter took all evening. Julie read it over repeatedly before she was satisfied. In the first paragraph, she thanked Roy for the good times they'd shared, for opening his home and his life to her for even this short while.

That had been the easy part of the letter. More difficult was discussing his utter rejection of her. Then she related her father's observation, telling Roy he could only trust her as much as he allowed himself to trust. In the last third of the letter, she apologized for her own angry response to his lack of faith.

It was midnight when she finished. Although she'd had trouble sleeping since their breakup, she experienced no such difficulty that night. Once again, she marveled at her father's wisdom. It really didn't matter whether or not Roy read her letter. In the process of articulating her reactions she'd found the peace she sought.

The next morning, the last day of school before winter break, Julie took the letter with her, planning to drop it off at the post office. School let out at noon, but after she'd had a festive lunch with the other teachers and straightened her classroom, it was nearly three. If she posted the letter as she'd originally intended, he might not receive it until after Christmas. She had no idea what his Christmas plans were; maybe he'd already left for a Caribbean cruise or a country inn in Vermont, she thought whimsically. At one time, she'd hoped to invite him and his mother to join her and her father. She hadn't even had the opportunity to broach the subject.

Nor had she spoken to his mother since Saturday. Anne hadn't called her, and Julie didn't feel comfortable putting his mother in the middle of this awkward situation.

Although it meant facing Jason, the guard at the entrance, she decided to deliver the letter personally.

Julie felt the guard's heated gaze on her the moment she pulled into the parking lot. His eyes didn't leave her until she'd parked in an empty slot and then climbed out of her car. Julie half expected the security guard to block the entrance. But Jason sat at his desk, one hand on the phone, obviously ready to call for reinforcements.

He reluctantly stood when she walked in, but remained solidly behind his desk, as if it afforded him protection.

"Stay away from me," Jason warned.

Startled, Julie glanced over her shoulder. No one else was there. She couldn't imagine why the burly guard would be afraid of *her*.

"I don't know what you did to me, lady, but I don't want a repeat of it, understand?"

"Jason," she said in her most conciliatory voice, "what in heaven's name are you talking about?"

"You know." He gestured theatrically. "Just stay right where you are. You're not allowed in this building."

Actually she'd expected that. "Not to worry, I don't have any intention of storming into Mr. Fletcher's office. I have a letter for him." She advanced slowly toward Jason's desk, not wanting to intimidate him any more than she already had, although how she'd done that was a mystery.

He backed away until he bumped into the wall behind him.

"All I ask is that you give Mr. Fletcher this letter," she said slowly, careful to enunciate every word. "You don't need to deliver it yourself," she assured him, in case it was an encounter with Roy that had unsettled him. "I'm sure Ms. Johnson will be more than happy to see that Mr. Fletcher receives it."

Jason's eyes moved past her and a chagrined expression appeared on his face.

Julie looked over her shoulder again to find Roy standing there. He'd clearly just stepped out of the elevator. Her first instinct, absurdly enough, was to turn tail and run. A second later, she seemed completely incapable of moving. Or breathing. Or anything else.

"What's Ms. Wilcoff doing in the building?" Roy asked the security guard as if Julie wasn't standing directly in front of him.

"She has a letter for you."

"Yes. I wrote you a letter." She hated the way her voice trembled, but she hadn't been prepared to see Roy. It wasn't supposed to happen like this!

Jason handed Roy the envelope, which he reluctantly accepted.

Julie's heart pounded in her ears. She had to escape as quickly as possible. "I'll leave now," she said.

"That would be best," Jason boomed. With his employer close at hand, he'd apparently regained his nerve. He stepped forward, arms akimbo, and escorted Julie to the front door, going so far as to push it open for her.

Julie felt Roy's eyes burning holes in her back as

she exited the building. She walked at twice her normal speed, intent on getting away.

Then she heard heavy footsteps behind her.

"What's in the letter?" Roy demanded, following her into the parking lot.

Julie fumbled for her car keys. "I suggest you read it." She stood by the driver's door, while Roy waited at the rear bumper.

"I imagine you declared your love and described how anguished you are by our parting."

Julie wasn't taking the bait. Everything she wanted to say was in the letter; she had no intention of repeating it and then arguing over the points she'd made.

"I'm not interested in the account of your undying love."

Her hand shook so badly she had trouble pressing the button to automatically unlock her car door.

"You're no different from Aimee." He seemed to want to provoke her into losing her temper. "What's the matter? Don't you have anything you want to say?"

A painful breath worked its way through her lungs. "Most everything is in the letter, Roy, but I realize now that there are a few things I left out."

"Good. You can say them to my face."

She studied him then, really looked at him, and saw how unhappy he was. This was the most joyous season of the year, and Roy was miserable.

"I didn't say I loved you," she said, her voice

gaining strength and control. ''As you'll discover if you read my letter.''

He arched his brow in that all-too-familiar sarcastic way.

''But the truth is, I do.''

''Spare me, please.''

''It's foolish, I suppose, but I always did like a challenge, and you, Roy Fletcher, are definitely that.'' She even managed a brief smile.

Again the sardonic arched brow.

''The thing is,'' she continued, determined not to let his cynicism destroy her, ''I do love you and it's up to you to accept that love or reject it.''

He said nothing.

''We haven't known each other long, but in that time, I've learned a great deal about the kind of man you are. You have a tremendous capacity to give of yourself, a tremendous capacity to love.'' She thought of the job he'd given her father and the fact that, unknown to his mother, he'd bought her paintings. She recalled the way he'd come to her soccer game—and so much more. His unpretentious enjoyment of her simple meals. The loyalty his staff had toward him...

He held up his hand. ''Not interested.''

''I know, and that saddens me, because I'm going to get in my car and drive away. I didn't come here to argue with you—I didn't even expect to see you.''

''It seems to me you planned it perfectly so you would.''

Did he honestly believe she'd somehow manipulated their simultaneous presence in the company foyer? "I didn't. But whether I did or not is of little concern."

He shrugged. Julie knew he must have some feelings for her, otherwise he wouldn't be standing with her now, wouldn't be listening to her. If this was her only chance to get through to him, then she might as well give it her best shot.

"You have the opportunity to decide what you want out of life, Roy. You can go on living behind your hard exterior, blocking out anyone who has the potential to teach you about love, or you can—"

"I already said I wasn't interested in love. I made that clear from the beginning," he snapped. "What is it with you? Every other word out of your mouth is some affirmation of love. Yeah, right! Well, I can't help wondering how much *love* you'd really feel if I wasn't who I am."

"Who are you, Roy?"

"You know what I mean," he said, and gestured to the building that stood as evidence of his prosperity.

"Are you the rich and successful entrepreneur?"

"You know what I mean," he repeated.

"Unfortunately, I don't," she said, opening her car door. "I thought I knew who you were, but I guess I was wrong."

"I thought I knew who *you* were," he retorted, his eyes blazing, "but you proved *me* wrong. All you care about is the size of my checking account and what you can get out of me."

She refused to listen to any more. With a heavy heart, she climbed inside the car.

"You're—"

She closed the door to drown out his words, then inserted the key into the ignition. When she glanced in her rearview mirror, Roy was gone.

Julie exited the parking lot, and as soon as she was out of sight, she pulled to the curb and wept tears of pain and grief.

Leaning her forehead against the steering wheel, she knew she'd never see Roy Fletcher again.

CHAPTER TWENTY-FOUR

"THIS IS ABSOLUTELY terrible," Goodness lamented. All afternoon, they'd watched Julie put on a good front for her father's sake. She could just picture the scene in Heaven when they returned only seven hours from now. It was Christmas Eve, their deadline. Soon they'd be required to stand with the angelic host singing praises to the newborn King. Except this year, Shirley, Goodness and Mercy would arrive from Earth without having fulfilled their mission. Goodness wouldn't be able to look a single friend in the face. Well, she wasn't accepting defeat that easily.

"It can't get much worse," Mercy agreed.

"We've got to do something." Shirley was back to her pacing in front of the Wilcoffs' Christmas tree. The living room was empty, with Julie in her room and Dean overseeing a last-minute security check of the Fletcher building.

"This is your fault," Goodness said, glaring at Mercy. "If you hadn't been so busy tossing salmon in Pike Place Market and holding security guards by the knees, we might've made some headway."

"Give it up," Mercy growled. "Besides, we both

know you had a hand on Jason, too. I couldn't have held him back all by myself. That guy has incredible muscles.''

''Stop.'' Shirley planted herself between the other two and shook her head. ''We don't have time to play the blame game.''

''You're telling me,'' Goodness moaned. ''It's already five o'clock.''

''That means we have seven paltry hours,'' Shirley said, glancing at the old-fashioned clock on the fireplace mantel.

''Woe is we.'' Goodness couldn't believe that a simple prayer request could go so wrong. They'd worked harder on this one than on any previous requests. In years past, they'd each received separate assignments, but she'd assumed that with their combined efforts this one would've been simplicity itself. Not so. And if there was anything Goodness hated, it was having to admit she'd failed. ''We've just *got* to do something.'' They had a few hours left. Just a few.

''But what?'' Mercy cried.

''Think,'' Shirley ordered. ''There's a way. There's always a way.''

Defeated and depressed, Goodness walked into the darkened kitchen and threw open the refrigerator door. For a long moment, she studied the contents. It was easy to understand why so many humans turned to food for comfort. A pan of something dipped in chocolate was bound to improve any situation.

"I had hope until Roy threw out her letter," Mercy said. "Without reading it."

"How could he?" Shirley asked, although the question was rhetorical. "I thought humans were curious about things." That was a characteristic they shared with angels.

"I'm sure he was tempted," Shirley said, sadness weighting her words. "However, his fear was even stronger."

"He was afraid?" Goodness was unable to decipher human reasoning. "Of what?"

"Of changing his mind," Shirley explained. "He knew if he read Julie's letter, he might be swayed. He couldn't let that happen. He couldn't hold on to his anger if he allowed himself to feel her love."

"But love is what he needs!"

Goodness wanted to weep with frustration. Shirley was right. Roy had closed himself off from love, even though he needed it, even though he wanted it. He equated love with pain. Opening his heart made him vulnerable, and he couldn't risk that after what his father and Aimee had done.

"I'd so hoped for a better outcome," Shirley murmured forlornly, "especially for Anne's sake."

"Anne," Goodness repeated, remembering Shirley's previous connection to Roy's mother. She studied the former Guardian Angel and detected a suspicious smile in her eyes. Quickly Shirley looked away.

"Shirley," Goodness pressed, certain now that

her friend was up to something, ''you're holding out on us.''

''Shirley?'' Mercy joined in. ''What did you do?''

A giggle escaped, followed by another. ''I made a quick trip to New York, and...well, you'll see soon enough.''

''Tell us!''

''And ruin the surprise?''

''Does it have to do with Roy and Julie?''

The laughter in Shirley's eyes quickly faded. ''Sorry, no.''

''With Anne?''

The humor was back and she nodded. ''All in good time, my friends, all in good time.''

''But what are we going to do about Roy and Julie?'' Even with the clock ticking away the last hours, Goodness refused to give up. Somehow or other, they *had* to accomplish their goal.

''That letter could always find its way back into his life,'' Goodness suggested. Which might mean a bit of detective work...

''I will serve the Lord with my whole heart,'' Mercy said, ''but I am not digging around in someone's garbage. That just isn't me.''

''You would if it meant we could answer this prayer request, wouldn't you?''

Mercy looked unsure. With her arms crossed, she cocked her head to one side and shrugged. ''Well...maybe.''

"Then let's get to it," Goodness cried with renewed hope. "We'll find the letter, *and* we'll make sure he reads it."

"How are we going to do that?" Shirley asked.

"We'll figure it out when the time comes," Mercy assured her. "You can't expect us to have all the answers, can you?"

"I don't expect all the answers," Goodness said, "but *one* answer would be nice."

"Why make things easy?" Mercy asked pertly.

"Right."

With renewed purpose the three hurried to Roy's condo. This was their last chance, and whatever happened, they had to make it work.

ROY PICKED UP the remote control and automatically flipped through the channels. He didn't stay on any one for more than a couple of seconds. His patience was nonexistent, and his irritation mounted by the moment. Roy didn't understand why he felt like this. He should be thrilled. His company had just had its best year to date. When any number of dot-com businesses were fast becoming dot-gone enterprises, his own was thriving. Money and happiness, however, didn't seem to be connected.

Roy had dreaded spending Christmas with his mother. Being continually reminded of everything she'd lost in the divorce was too much for him, especially during the holiday season. Pretending was beyond him. Now she was in New York with her college friend and he could do as he pleased.

Only nothing pleased him.

"What did you do in other years?" he asked himself out loud.

Work had dominated his life for so long that he had no idea what it meant to relax. Christmas Eve should be special in some way, except it wasn't. If he was with Julie, it would be… He refused to think about Julie. She was out of his life and he was out of hers. Good. That was exactly how he wanted it.

With nothing on television to intrigue him, Roy sat down at his computer. Because he felt he should know what was going on in the world, he left the local news channel playing in the background. He decided to surf the Internet. Maybe he'd get so wrapped up investigating Web sites that the evening would vanish without his realizing where all those hours had gone; it had happened often enough before. Then he could forget that it was Christmas Eve, forget he was alone.

That didn't seem to work, either.

No Web site interested him for more than a few minutes.

"A Christmas story of generosity that's guaranteed to touch everyone's heart," the newscaster said from behind him. "Details after a word from our sponsors."

Roy was in no mood to be cheered by anyone's generosity. He turned around to reach for the remote and turn off the TV. Love and goodwill were not in keeping with his current mood.

The remote was missing.

It had been on the coffee table just a moment ago and now it was nowhere in sight. He started lifting papers and cushions in his search, but he always kept it in the same place on the coffee table. It was gone.

A sentimental commercial about a college student arriving home on Christmas Eve began to play. It was a sappy ad, meant to tug at the heartstrings. Roy had never liked it. He groaned and renewed his search for the remote.

Then the female newscaster was back. ''Tonight we have the story of a single gift of twenty-five thousand dollars donated anonymously at a Salvation Army bell station.''

The scene changed to one outside a local shopping mall. Cars whizzed past as the camera zoomed toward a lone figure standing in front of a big red pot. Dressed in his overcoat and muffler, a scarf tied around his neck, the volunteer diligently rang his bell, reminding everyone that there were others less fortunate this Christmas season.

Roy continued his search with one eye on the television screen. He knew he should simply lean over and hit the power switch, but for some reason, he didn't.

''An anonymous donor came up to Gary Wilson yesterday afternoon and slipped a cashier's check for twenty-five thousand dollars into his collection canister. This is the largest single donation a Salvation Army bell ringer has ever received in our area.''

Roy froze, rooted to the spot, his quest for the TV remote forgotten.

''Gary, can you tell us anything about the person who gave you that check?'' the reporter asked, shoving a microphone in front of the volunteer's face.

The poor man looked like a deer caught on the freeway, lights coming at him from every direction. ''No,'' he finally blurted. ''I didn't notice anyone who seemed rich enough to give away that kind of money.''

The reporter spoke into the microphone again. ''That money will go a long way toward making this Christmas a happy one for a lot of community families, won't it?'' Once more she thrust the microphone at the Salvation Army volunteer.

''I think it was a woman,'' Gary Wilson said. ''It was about the middle of my shift, I'd say. Things were moving pretty briskly and then this tall gal came up.'' He paused. ''She said Merry Christmas, and she smiled. But I don't know if it was her or not. It could've been.'' He punctuated his comments with a shrug. ''Or maybe not. Could've been that short fellow who refused to look me in the eye. Real short, he was.''

''Elf-size?'' the reporter asked with a grin.

Gary nodded. ''Yup, elf-size.''

"Well, it looks like Santa won't have to work nearly as hard in the Seattle area this year. Back to you, Jean."

"Thank you, Tracy," the female announcer said.

Roy sank onto the edge of his plush leather sofa. It was Julie; she *had* to be the "tall gal" the volunteer had mentioned. This was a calculated move on her part. She'd…

His thoughts ground to a halt. Julie hadn't done it for the publicity. With a cashier's check, she wasn't expecting to be honored for the donation. The truth was, Roy couldn't prove that it'd been her. But it seemed more than a coincidence that the donation was the same amount as the check he'd given her.

Leaning back, he rubbed his face, then glanced at the coffee table. To his utter amazement, there sat the remote control. He looked again, harder. Nah, couldn't be. He leaned forward. It hadn't been there a moment ago. That wasn't the only thing on the coffee table, either.

There sat Julie's letter.

This was the same envelope he'd recently discarded. The same envelope with his name carefully written on the front in Julie's smooth and even cursive hand.

Roy gasped, leaped up and quickly looked around. Something very strange was happening.

He'd been working too hard, he decided, brushing the hair away from his forehead. He left his hand resting there as he tried to reason this out in his troubled mind.

The pressure had become too much for him. That was it. What had been wrong a few minutes ago now seemed perfectly logical. What was left was now right. What was top was now bottom.

The envelope seemed to glow, daring him to open it. When he'd originally received the letter, the temptation to read it had been almost overwhelming. But instead, Roy had tossed it in the garbage as soon as he got home. Then, because he couldn't get it out of his mind, he'd taken the garbage from his kitchen and carried it to the chute in the utility room. The chute deposited all garbage in a Dumpster in the basement.

Yet here was the letter, back in his possession.

"Obviously I should read it," he muttered to himself, certain he should be looking for the phone number of a psychiatrist first. This couldn't be happening. But it was.

Sinking back onto the couch, he reached for the letter. He didn't *want* to read it, yet from the first word on, he felt compelled to continue. His cynicism gradually eroded as he recognized her sincerity with every sentence. He understood her exasperation with him and respected the honesty and integrity that underlined her actions, her beliefs. The most powerful of all the emotions that washed over him as he read her letter was love. *Her* love.

Earlier, she'd told him she hadn't written that she loved him, but he felt it in every word.

After reading the letter once, he set it aside and tried to absorb everything she'd said. Then he read it again, more slowly this time, sometimes rereading a sentence twice.

"She's right," he whispered. "She's so right." He'd been given this chance. The most wonderful gift of his life was right in front of him and he was rejecting it. He could allow what Aimee had done to taint the rest of his days, or he could move forward.

Christmas Eve, and he was alone. But he didn't have to be.

He could spend Christmas with Julie.

Christmas and every other day.

A surge of joy rushed through him. He wasn't waiting a moment longer.

CHAPTER TWENTY-FIVE

FOR HER FATHER'S SAKE, Julie made the effort to see that this first Christmas without her mother was as cheerful as she could make it. For dinner on Christmas Eve, Julie served the meal her mother had always prepared. A big pot of homemade clam chowder simmered on the stove and a loaf of freshly baked bread waited on the counter. Although she didn't have much of an appetite, Julie was determined to sit down, smile and enjoy their evening together. Letty had phoned earlier, and Julie had done her best to sound optimistic. She didn't know how well she'd succeeded.

"Something smells mighty good," her father said as he stepped into the kitchen. He lifted the lid from the large pot and offered Julie a smile. "Your mother's recipe?"

She nodded.

Her father closed his eyes and breathed in the scent of the chowder. "I feel that she's with us."

"I do, too, Dad."

"For the first time since she died, I feel her presence more profoundly than I do her absence. I'm sure it has to do with Christmas."

"I'm sure it does, too."

"She was such a Christmas person."

Her father wasn't telling Julie anything she didn't know. The house was always beautifully decorated for the holidays. Her mother spent endless hours seeing to every detail. Even her Christmas cards were special—because she wrote individual messages to each person. She baked and cooked for weeks beforehand, and every December she gave their neighbors gifts of homemade cookies and candies. Julie had made an attempt to do the same, but she didn't have the time, the patience or the skill to match her mother's efforts. Her lone batch of fudge was a humbling experience and she ditched it before her father got home to see what a mess she'd made.

"Everything's ready," she announced. Instead of eating in the kitchen as they routinely did at night, they were using the dining room. After dinner and the dishes, they'd be ready for Christmas Eve services at church.

"I'll bring out the chowder," her father said as the doorbell rang.

Julie frowned. "Are you expecting anyone?"

Her father shook his head. "I'll get it."

While her father dealt with whoever was at the door, Julie ladled the soup into the tureen her mother had saved for special occasions. The bread, a recipe handed down for more than three generations, was a holiday tradition, too. Julie could recall how her mother had called Letty and Julie to the kitchen table and taught them the importance of kneading the dough. They'd loved doing it.

"It appears we have company," her father said from behind her.

Julie turned around. Had there been anything in her hands, it would have crashed to the floor.

Roy Fletcher stood beside her father, his arms full of gifts, which he arranged under the tree.

"I'll set an extra place at the table," Dean said as though it was a foregone conclusion that Roy would be joining them.

Julie was cemented to the floor. Had her life depended on it, she couldn't have moved. "What are you doing here?" she choked out.

"I read your letter."

Better late than never, she wanted to tell him, but speaking had become somewhat difficult.

"Oh."

"It was a beautiful letter."

Her father walked past Julie. "The two of you can sort everything out after dinner. You will stay, won't you, Roy?"

"Yes. Thank you, Dean...." He nodded, although the entire time he was speaking, he kept his eyes on Julie.

"Come on." Her father urged them toward the dining room.

As if in a dream, Julie left the kitchen. Roy held out her chair for her, and her father placed the soup tureen in the center of the table. He hurried back to the kitchen for the bread. When they were all gathered at the table, they joined hands for grace.

Julie bowed her head and closed her eyes. She'd prayed for this, prayed Roy would feel her love, prayed he'd know she was sincere. Still, there was a sense of unreality about tonight. Her father's words, asking God to bless their meal, barely registered in her mind. At the sound of his "Amen," she lifted her head to discover Roy watching her. Her breathing stopped at the unmistakable love she saw in his eyes. She didn't understand what had happened to him, but whatever it was had completely changed him. Or, more accurately, made him the person he was meant to be. The person he really was.

"Your coming by is a pleasant surprise," her father said conversationally as he stood and reached for Roy's bowl.

"I should've phoned first," Roy said, and his gaze, which had been on Julie, moved to her father. "I hope it isn't an imposition." His eyes returned to her.

"Not at all. Julie made plenty. You do like clam chowder, don't you?"

"Yes, very much." Again his eyes briefly left her. "Julie and I had clam chowder the first time we went to dinner."

"At an old college hangout of Roy's," she added.

Roy smiled.

"Julie baked the bread this evening," her father said proudly as he reached for Julie's soup bowl next. "It's her mother's recipe. She did an excellent job of it, too."

Julie passed the bread basket to Roy.

"It's an old German recipe. Her mother was of German ancestry," Dean went on to explain.

"I'm sure it's excellent."

"It is," her father continued. "Julie's mother was an exceptional woman." He ladled soup into his own bowl and then sat down.

Her hands shaking, Julie offered Roy the butter.

Her father apparently wasn't finished. "Darlene used to say it was a couple's duty to keep their eyes open, their ears open, their hearts open and their mouths shut." He laughed robustly.

Roy grinned.

Julie was following that bit of advice at the moment. She couldn't possibly have carried on a civil conversation. All she could think about was the fact that Roy was in her home, sharing Christmas Eve dinner with her father and her. As far as she was concerned, this was nothing short of a miracle.

"I hope you'll attend church services with us later." Her father turned to Roy.

"I'd be delighted."

"My wife had a lot of wonderful sayings," he murmured, reverting to his previous topic. "She said interruptions were simply God's appointments."

"I interrupted you this evening," Roy said.

"Now, Dad..." All this talk about her mother and God would probably confuse Roy. Christmas Eve was not the time to eulogize her mother. Then it occurred to Julie that her father needed to do this, that he wanted to remember and honor her by sharing her favorite expressions.

"Please go on," Roy said. "I'd like to hear some of the other things your wife said."

Her father grinned and set down his spoon. "My wife firmly believed that God sends pain into our lives for a reason."

Roy frowned. "That's an interesting thought. Most people don't think of God in terms of pain."

"I know," Dean said. "Now, Roy, I realize from what Julie's told me that you've seen more than your fair share of emotional turmoil. I don't mean to discount that, but my wife always said we should lean into the pain, instead of running away from it."

"Like driving into a skid in order to correct it?" Roy suggested.

"Exactly," Dean crowed. "We have to *use* the experience. We can become either bitter or better."

Julie wasn't sure where her father was going with this conversation. "Daddy?"

"She only calls me that when she's upset."

"It's okay, Julie. I want to hear this," Roy said.

"Good, because I think it's something you need to hear." Her father had given up all pretense of eating. "Now it seems to me that you're interested in my little girl."

Julie was sure her cheeks were flaming. All this spiritual talk wasn't like her father, who kept his faith private. She couldn't imagine why he was saying the things he was.

"I care a great deal for Julie," Roy confessed.

Julie nearly dropped her spoon. As it was, the utensil clattered against the china bowl.

Roy glanced at her. "Unfortunately, it took me a while to understand what I was doing."

"So it seems." Her father gestured grandly with a piece of bread. "But all's well that ends well, right?"

"Right." He turned to meet Julie's eyes. "You're the one who anonymously donated that twenty-five thousand dollars to the Salvation Army, aren't you?"

Julie went very still. "Is that why you're here?"

"No, but it was a catalyst. The bell—so to speak—that woke me up."

"How did you know?" She'd done it anonymously for a reason.

"You haven't seen the news, have you?"

Julie was aghast. "It was on the evening news?"

"Channel Four."

"I watched Channel Four earlier and didn't see anything about it," her father said.

"It was there," Roy insisted. "They interviewed a man by the name of Gary Wilson, a volunteer stationed at the Alderwood Mall." He looked at Julie. "It *was* you who gave that check to the Salvation Army, wasn't it?"

For a second, she considered misleading him, then decided against it. "Would it matter?"

Roy thought for a moment, then shook his head. "No. I don't care what you did with the money because I know in my heart that you love me."

"Those are mighty sweet words," her father said, grinning from ear to ear.

"Dad!"

"Now, Roy, you say you care for Julie. Does that mean you love her?"

"Dad!" she cried again. She couldn't believe that her father would ask such a thing, especially with her sitting right there.

"I love her."

"Good," her father said nonchalantly, as if men regularly talked this way at the dining room table.

Roy chuckled, but Julie spoke before he could say anything else. "Would you two kindly involve me in this conversation?"

"She's right," Roy agreed.

"Now *I'll* be the one to say those are some mighty sweet words," Julie muttered. It was the first time she could remember Roy admitting she was right about anything.

"I should warn you," her father said, leaning toward him. "She's got a stubborn streak."

"I know all about it," Roy whispered back.

Julie rolled her eyes. "Who are you calling stubborn?"

"Well," her father said. "Enough squabbling. Now if you two will excuse me, I'll get ready for church."

Julie didn't stop him although there was at least an hour before they needed to leave. She heard him turn on the radio in his room, presumably to give them greater privacy.

All of a sudden Julie and Roy were sitting at the dining room table alone. She wanted to remind him of his claim that he wasn't interested in love—and then remembered her mother's saying about keeping her ears open and her mouth shut. Good advice, and for once she planned on taking it.

"You don't have anything you want to say?" Roy asked, and for the first time he seemed unsure of himself.

"I was about to ask you the same thing."

Roy took her hand and clasped it tightly. "This might not make a whole lot of sense, but I feel as though I got specific orders to come here tonight."

"Orders from whom? Your mother?"

"No... I have no idea who sent me, but I know beyond a doubt that I was supposed to be here."

Her heart began to beat faster. "Did you want to come?"

"More than anything, Julie, only I didn't realize it. I was doing what your mother said—running away from the pain."

"Oh, how I wish you'd known her."

"I think I already do," he said. "I know *you,* Julie, and I know that your heart is good and that you have a gift for reaching out to others."

She looked away, uncomfortable with his compliments.

"I know you aren't influenced by money and that I can trust you with my heart."

"Your heart?" she repeated, her voice low and unsteady.

"I once asked you to move in with me."

Her throat started to close again, and she found it almost impossible to speak. "Is that why you're here?" she managed.

"No. I can say that was a mistake. I want to make you a permanent part of my life."

"Are...are you asking me to marry you?"

His fingers tightened around hers. "That would be a good place to start."

"You mean there's more?"

He chuckled. "About fifty years more, I'd say. Longer, if we're lucky. I'd like to begin our new life soon. Is that all right by you?"

"Children?"

He nodded. "A dozen, at least."

"Roy, be serious!"

"All right, two or three, whatever we decide when the time comes. My mother's anxious for grandchildren and I wouldn't dream of disappointing her."

This was all happening so fast Julie wasn't sure she could keep up.

A strangled ringing sound startled her; she looked around.

"It's my cell," Roy said, removing it from his pocket. He flipped the tiny phone open and glanced at the number. "My mother. I can't imagine why she's calling me this late. It's after eleven in New York."

"Answer it," Julie said. "We have some pretty wonderful news."

He looked at her expectantly.

Julie smiled. "You can tell her I've accepted your marriage proposal."

Roy's eyes were warm and loving as he reached for her with one hand, pushing the talk button on his cell phone with the other.

This was the most wonderful Christmas Eve of her life, and Julie gave silent thanks.

Was it a coincidence that "Hark the Herald Angels Sing" began to play on the radio at that very moment?

CHAPTER TWENTY-SIX

"ROY! OH, ROY!" Anne was so excited she could barely speak. "In a million years you won't believe what's happened."

"I have some pretty incredible news of my own," he said.

Despite her preoccupation with her own joy, Anne could hear the happiness in her son's voice. "Tell me," she said, unable to wait a moment longer for his news.

"Julie has agreed to be my wife."

Tears of joy instantly pricked Anne's eyes. This was much more wonderful than she'd dared dream. "That's marvelous!"

"We haven't set a date, but I know it'll be soon. I've been waiting my entire life for her, Mom. I can't believe what a fool I was all this time. You must have wanted to throw up your hands."

"I prayed that God would send a special woman into your life," she admitted. Although her prayer had been sincere, she'd almost given up hope. Coping with her own problems, struggling to keep her head above water financially, Anne had tried hard to help her son. It had seemed hopeless for so long, she'd lost confidence that any woman was capable of touching his heart. And then he met Julie....

"Let me put her on the phone," Roy said.

"Yes, please." Anne felt so full of happiness she was practically overwhelmed. So much good news, and all at once.

"Anne..." Julie's tentative voice came over Anne's cell phone.

"Julie, Merry Christmas!" Anne burst out. "Roy gave me this phone for Christmas, and you're the first call I've made on it. I always thought of them as a damn nuisance, but tonight it's worth its weight in gold. I understand my son's finally come to his senses and asked you to marry him."

"He did and it didn't take me long to answer him, either."

"You're going to be a beautiful bride and exactly the wife he needs."

"Thank you—I certainly plan to try. I feel so blessed."

"Oh, me, too," Anne said fervently.

"Let me give the phone back to Roy."

Anne could hear soft, loving sounds as the phone was transferred back to her son. "All right, Mother," Roy said, "I'm glad you're using your new phone. Now tell me your news."

"You won't believe this," she said again, and because she couldn't help it, she broke into giggles.

"Then tell me," Roy said.

"My painting of the angel sold."

"Congratulations! From the excitement in your voice, it must have been for a lot of money. The last I heard, you thought it might go for as much as twenty-five thousand."

"Try a hundred and fifty."

"What?"

"A bidding war drove up the price, but that's not the best part."

"What's the best part? What could possibly be better than that?"

"Oh, Roy, just you wait until I tell you *who* bought the painting." She paused, relishing the justice of it. "The check was written by Burton Fletcher. Your father."

Her announcement was followed by shocked silence.

"Why would Dad write you a check for that amount of money?" Roy finally asked.

"First," Anne explained, "he didn't know it was me."

"But—"

"Since I paint under the name of Mary Flemming, your father had no way of knowing that the woman who painted the angel was his ex-wife. Marta knew, of course, and she already had someone else interested, so she was able to use the other interested party to drive up the price."

"Go back to the beginning," Roy said.

"Marta—you remember my college friend who runs an art gallery here in New York?"

"Yes, yes, of course I remember her. You're staying at her place. Go on with your story."

"Well, when she shipped the painting to New York and hung it in the gallery, she put up a sign that said it wasn't for sale. But then Aimee came into the gallery and fell in love with it."

"Aimee," Roy repeated. "When she stopped by the office, she'd obviously been on a recent shopping spree. And, of course, there was her bargain with Dad—a phone call from me in exchange for…your painting, as it turns out."

"She wanted my angel in the worst way."

"And Dad actually forked out that kind of money to buy it for her."

"He did," Anne said, unable to keep the laughter from her voice. "But he had no idea he was giving me a big chunk of what I should've gotten in the first place. He cheated me with the divorce settlement and now…"

"You always did say that what goes around comes around," Roy said, sounding as delighted as she was. "I think that painting must be something special."

"Thank you, Roy. I do, too, but I never *dreamed* it would sell for such an outrageous amount of money."

"Does Dad know yet?" her son asked.

"I'm not telling him." Although it was tempting

to do so, Anne had resisted. "I suspect that sooner or later he'll discover it on his own."

"Yes, I suppose he will. I'd love to be a fly on the wall when he figures it out."

"There's more good news," Anne said, hardly able to contain herself. "Marta said that she could sell as many angel paintings as I want to paint. There seems to be a real demand for them now. I think I've finally found my niche."

"That's great, Mom."

Her son seemed genuinely pleased for her. "I'm thinking of painting one for you and Julie as a wedding gift. It certainly seems to me that we've all had angels watching over us."

"We'd like that very much."

"Marta and her husband—"

"I thought they'd separated."

Anne had nearly forgotten. With so much else happening, her friend's news had slipped her mind. "Jack and Marta are back together. Jack *was* seeing someone else, but apparently it wasn't as serious as Marta assumed. They're going to a counselor and are determined to work on their marriage."

"That's good news."

"Life just seems to get better and better," Anne said, sighing softly, tired now and elated at the same time.

"Yes, indeed it does," her son agreed. "Better and better."

"WE DID IT!" Goodness was thrilled. Leaping up and down in the choir loft at the First Christian

Church of North Seattle, she didn't even try to sit still. The church was rapidly filling as families streamed in from the vestibule.

Roy, Julie and Dean walked into the crowded sanctuary and found seats near the front. They were too late to find a pew in the back, where Dean preferred to sit.

"Isn't the altar lovely?" Shirley said with a sigh, pointing toward the poinsettias arranged around the table that held the Advent wreath. All four candles were lit, their flames flickering, little dances of delight.

"I wouldn't believe it if I hadn't seen Roy propose to Julie with my own eyes," Mercy said with satisfaction. "I have to tell you, scenes like this always get to me."

"Do they now," Gabriel said from behind them.

Shirley, Goodness and Mercy whirled around to face the Archangel. Goodness held her breath, certain Gabriel was going to chastise them for their earthly manipulations. They'd become far more involved in the things of the world than ever before, but surely Gabriel had made allowances on their behalf, knowing the challenge they'd had with Roy.

"Did you see Roy and Julie?" Goodness pointed. The proof of their success was sitting directly below.

"I did," Gabriel said, and nodded approvingly. "I must say you used some unconventional methods to fulfill your mission. Tell me, what did Roy learn from all this?"

A prayer couldn't be answered unless there was a lesson learned.

"His lesson was about love," Shirley answered. "His mother's love touched him. Her prayers for her son were heard by all of Heaven, and God sent us to show Roy that he *could* find love."

"Very good," Gabriel said. "But then, you always knew that, didn't you, Shirley?"

The former Guardian Angel nodded. "I did. Anne was such a special child. I always knew she'd grow up to be a special woman, and I was right."

"Can you give us a peek into the future?" Mercy asked, crowding between Goodness and Shirley in an effort to gain Gabriel's attention.

"Yes, please." Goodness added her request.

Only a few were given the privilege of gazing into the future, and Gabriel was one.

"Tell me about Anne," Shirley pleaded.

"Your Anne will continue to paint for a number of productive years."

"Angels?"

"Yes, and landscapes. The fees she earns from the angel paintings will support her far and above what she ever imagined. She'll become well-known for her work. In the years ahead, she will be recognized as a fine and talented artist. People will pay high prices to own one of Mary Flemming's paintings."

"I'm so glad," Shirley said happily.

"And to think it all started with you," Goodness said to her. The instant the words were out, she realized what she'd done—alerted Gabriel to the fact that Shirley had appeared to Anne. She clapped both hands over her mouth.

Gabriel, fortunately, didn't seem to notice her slip.

"What about Burton and Aimee?" Mercy asked.

Gabriel's sigh was heavy. "They'll divorce in two years when she leaves him for another man. Burton will be stunned and hurt. He becomes something of a recluse after that. Over time, Roy and his father will reconcile and the greatest joy of his life will become his grandchildren."

"I'm so sorry to hear his marriage to Aimee didn't turn out the way he expected."

"Burton was a man who brokered misery," Gabriel reminded them. "He brought about his own unhappiness."

"He always discounted Anne," Shirley said. "And to think that because of him, she'll become a famous artist."

"What about Roy and Julie? Will they be happy?" Goodness asked, decidedly pleased with her efforts.

"Very much so," Gabriel said, brightening. "Their marriage will be a good one. In the next five years, Julie will give birth to three children, two boys and a girl. All three will be athletic and intelligent. Their daughter, named Anne Darlene after her two grandmothers, will go on to be an Olympic swimmer. The boys will take after their father and eventually assume leadership of Fletcher Enterprises.''

''What about Dean?''

Gabriel sighed. ''He'll retire in a few years and then die peacefully in his sleep.''

''So he'll be joining his wife in Heaven a few Earth-years from now.''

''Yes,'' Gabriel replied. ''Are you satisfied now?''

Shirley, Goodness and Mercy nodded.

''Ready?'' he asked. In the distance, Goodness heard the strains of the heavenly choir as the angels gathered together to sing praise to the newborn King. But before she left Earth, Goodness had to know about Anne's mother. She just had to know.

Shirley stepped close to her side. ''She was an artist, too, and a wonderful mother. I always had a soft spot in my heart for Anne and wanted to work with her after her mother's death. God had other purposes for me, but He allowed me back into Anne's life for just this short time. I'm very grateful.''

So was Goodness.

The strains of the heavenly choir were richer and more distinct as the four of them drew closer. Ah, but this was a special night on Earth, one filled with glory and goodwill toward mankind. A night that came only once a year when God smiled down on those He loved and sent His angels to shout out the glad news.

Welcome to Koomera Crossing,
a town hidden deep in the Australian Outback.
Let renowned romance novelist Margaret Way
take you there. Let her introduce you to
the people of Koomera Crossing.
Let her tell you their secrets....

Watch for

Home to Eden,

available from Harlequin Superromance
in February 2004.

And don't miss the other Koomera Crossing books:

Sarah's Baby
(Harlequin Superromance #1111, February 2003)

Runaway Wife
(Harlequin Romance, October 2003)

Outback Bridegroom
(Harlequin Romance, November 2003)

Outback Surrender
(Harlequin Romance, December 2003)

Visit us at www.eHarlequin.com HSRKOOM